fiction

Please return this item to any Poole library by the due date.
Renew on (01202) 265200 or at
www.boroughofpoole.com/libraries

boroughofpoole.com

After a long and successful career in the pulp and paper industry, during which he visited 68 countries on 5 continents and lived for seven years in the USA and a year in the Bahamas, British author Malcolm Roscow now lives ~~~~~~~ ~~~~~~~ ~~~ ~~~~~~ his time keeping fi

I dedicate this novel to my late wife, Eileen, the mother of my children and the love of my life. You may be gone, my darling, but you'll never be forgotten.

Malcolm Roscow

ANOTHER BORING DAY IN PARADISE

AUSTIN MACAULEY
PUBLISHERS LTD.

A CIP catalogue record for this title is available from the British Library.

Author portrait artwork by Andrew Callaghan.

ISBN 978 1 78455 425 5

www.austinmacauley.com

First Published (2015)
Austin Macauley Publishers Ltd.
25 Canada Square
Canary Wharf
London
E14 5LB

Printed and bound in Great Britain

Freeport, Bahamas, 1992 –

It was a typical Bahamian summer's evening: temperature in the mid eighties, humidity close to ninety percent. There was no wind, not even enough to cause a flicker in the citronella candles on the balcony tables. A gentle swell on the edge of the Atlantic Ocean, a mere ten feet below the balcony, lapped the rocks and the stilts upon which the restaurant was built.

Pier One was Grand Bahama's best-known seafood restaurant and the best tables were on the balcony. Out there, patrons got the best view of the nightly shark-feeding extravaganza.

A Carnival Lines cruise ship was tied up in the docks a couple of hundred yards away. It dwarfed everything in sight. The vessel was docked rear-end to the restaurant; displaying MIAMI as its port of registration.

Liz had put on a knee-length red cocktail dress. John had bought it for her on a business trip to Zurich, and she knew he loved to see her wearing it. She wanted to look her very best for him. She was missing him terribly and was desperately hoping he would turn up tonight. At least she knew now that he was still alive.

She was sitting at a table by the balcony rail with George and Jill Humphries when Sybille arrived. She was laughing at a joke George had just told them. George was doing his level best to keep her amused; he knew only too well how distressed she had been since John had gone missing. Her smile froze when she saw Sybille, although she was not at all surprised to see her, because she had long since figured out what the click on the line had meant when Jill had phoned her.

Sybille was with a tall, elegant man in a well-cut suit. His hair was dark and his skin was swarthy. To Liz, he looked South American, and knowing that Sybille was involved in trafficking drugs, that was probably a safe bet. Sybille was carrying a large manila envelope.

When Sybille had learned that Liz would be dining at Pier One, she had phoned Uwe and insisted on being given the next table. Uwe had protested that he was fully booked and did not have a table available, but Sybille was having none of it. And Uwe knew better than to argue with Sybille. He was now escorting her, and her companion, to their table.

Sybille stopped at Liz's table and smiled mockingly at her. "Well fancy meeting you here."

"Very funny," Liz said coldly.

Sybille laughed. She walked to her table. Uwe pulled out a chair for her.

She sat down and her escort followed suit. Uwe handed them menus and told Sybille he would send over the drinks waiter.

As Uwe walked back past Liz's table, Humphries caught his arm. "Uwe," he said quietly, "can you give us another table? I don't want Liz to have to sit so close to that Johanssen woman."

George Humphries was one of Uwe's best customers and under normal circumstances he would have been delighted to oblige, but he was always fully booked when a cruise ship was in port, and Sybille had taken his last table. As it was, in order to please Sybille, Uwe had had to disappoint another regular customer who had specifically asked for a table on the balcony to impress the lady he was dining with. He was now sitting in the main body of the restaurant with a face the length of a wet weekend. "I'm sorry, Mr Humphries," Uwe said. "I would if I could, but all my tables are taken."

"Don't worry about it, Uwe," Liz said. "I'll be fine here."

She patted Humphries' arm. "It's all right, George. She can't get up to any mischief with all these people around."

Liz was about to make a start on her lobster thermidor when Sybille tapped her on the shoulder. They were sitting back-to-back, about eighteen inches apart.

Liz frowned and turned. "What is it, Sybille?"

Sybille thrust the manila envelope at her. "Here, read it, and sign it."

Taken by surprise, Liz took the envelope. "What is it for heaven's sake?"

"The agreement."

"What agreement?"

"Come off it, Liz. You promised to sign an agreement, and here it is. So sign the goddamn thing."

Liz tossed the agreement back. "In your dreams, Sybille."

"You'll sign it before the night's out," Sybille said. "And that's a promise."

DCI Johnson of the Freeport police hammered on the door of Sybille's apartment. "Police! Open the door!" There was no reply. He hammered again. "Come on, Sybille. We know you're in there."

A woman of extremely generous proportions, and wearing a voluminous dressing gown and enormous pink curlers in her hair, had heard the commotion and had stepped out of the adjoining apartment. "Are you looking for that *Johanssen* woman?" The way she spat out Sybille's name left no room for argument as to what she thought of Sybille.

"Yes, and we're in a hurry," Johnson snapped. "Any idea where she might be?"

"Try Pier One," the woman said. "And when you catch up with the rude bitch, do me a favour and throw away the key."

Dusk was rapidly approaching and the lights in the main body of the restaurant had been turned on. Fresh citronella candles, to provide both illumination and to keep the mosquitoes at bay, had been lit on the tables on the balcony.

Uwe walked out of the restaurant with a fish box full of frozen whitebait. He rested the box on the balcony rail immediately behind George Humphries, and, with his free hand, flicked a switch on a stanchion supporting the balcony roof. Powerful underwater searchlights cast a ghostly swathe of pale green light across a large area of water.

Affixed to the same stanchion was a ship's bell, and Uwe rang it eight times. *Ding ding, ding ding, ding ding, ding ding.* The sound echoed across the water.

It was show time, and there was a mad scramble for the balcony rail as people rushed to watch the show. Those fortunate enough to be sitting at tables on the balcony, also got to their feet and hurried to the rail. They knew only too well that there would soon be such a crush that unless they got to the rail quickly, the only thing they would see would be other people's backs.

Liz had seen it all before, but she never tired of this, and even though she was sitting next to the balcony rail, she pushed her chair back and jumped to her feet.

Sybille heard Liz move, and jumped to her feet. She stood to Liz's right. Their shoulders were touching. There was nothing either of them could do about it, because there was now such a crush at the rail that they couldn't have moved if they had tried.

Uwe grabbed a handful of the frozen fish in the box and tossed it over the rail. The sound of it splattering into the water below was heard by all and sundry, because there was now complete silence. He tossed over another handful, then another, then another. Then he up-ended the box, emptying the rest of its contents into the water. Then he turned to go for another box.

The crowd parted good-naturedly to let him through.

Down below, shoals of small fish darted out of the black water and into the circle of light and began to feed on the bait. It was a feeding frenzy, albeit not on big scale. Yet!

Uwe came back with another box and again the crowd parted to let him through. This time, he up-ended the box immediately, contents splattering into the water. The feeding frenzy paused, as the fish scattered, but before Uwe had come back with yet another box, they were back and gorging themselves again.

Again, Uwe upended the box, and again, they scattered.

Uwe put the box down against the balcony rail and stood there to watch. His food was good, excellent even, but this was the reason the punters came. He put on this show seven nights a week, fifty weeks of the year. The show would never be allowed in most civilised countries, because there was no net, nothing to prevent people falling over the rail.

There was movement from the edge of the circle of light and people craned their necks to see what it was. Barracuda were taking an interest. They began to emerge into the circle of light, cautiously. Soon there were a couple of dozen or more, some upwards of five feet long. They assumed positions around the edge of the circle of light, and lay motionless, like sharpened logs. Suddenly, as if on a signal from a leader, they barrelled in. Their prey scattered, but they were not fast enough, and the water began to roil as the ocean greyhounds began their evening feast.

A dorsal fin appeared.

A man's voice yelled, "There's one."

A woman's voice shouted, "There's another one."

Within a matter of minutes, upwards of a dozen sharks were circling. People at the rail were excitedly identifying reef sharks, tiger sharks, hammerheads and makos.

The flash photography was reminiscent of film stars arriving at a movie premier.

The sound of approaching police sirens could be heard faintly over the din.

The sharks circled faster and faster, and then launched themselves into the melee. Now, the hunters – the barracuda – were the hunted. There were shrieks of delight from the spectators as the water boiled and the sharks ripped into their prey, their mouths gaping and their teeth bloody.

The sirens were getting louder.

Sybille elbowed Liz in the ribs and thrust the agreement at her. "Here, sign the fucking thing."

Liz snatched the agreement off her and tossed it over the rail. "I'm not signing anything, you stupid woman. He's still alive."

Momentarily unable to take on board what Liz had done, Sybille watched her precious agreement, a straightforward one-page document, floating serenely down towards the water. And then she reacted ...

Chapter 2

"John, this is positively the last time you drag me off to another country. If you don't find what you're looking for in the Bahamas, I'm going straight back to England, with, or without you. Do I make myself clear?"

"Yes, dear," John said.

"Don't *yes dear* me, John, I mean it. You know I don't want to leave Florida. I love it here."

"I know, Liz, and I'm sorry. I really am."

"And why do you need to make more money, anyway. Surely, we have enough."

"Liz, I'm fifty, and I need to do something useful with my life. And, anyway, I'm sure you'd rather live in the Bahamas than go back and suffer the English weather. I know I would."

Their conversation was interrupted by the announcement that their flight to Freeport was now open for boarding.

John got the tickets and passports ready. "Do you want a window seat, if I can get you one?"

"John, I don't care where I sit. Just get me a seat."

John walked to the Comair check-in desk and handed over their documents. The porter followed him with their luggage.

The desk attendant flipped through their British passports and extracted the I-94 immigration forms. She frowned. "Do you realise you're in the United States illegally? Your visas expired a month ago."

John was well aware of it. That was one of the reasons they were leaving. He shifted uncomfortably.

The attendant turned to a colleague at the next desk. "Ted, these I-94s have expired. Do I need to inform immigration?"

Her colleague peered over his glasses at John – a tall, well-built man wearing a double-breasted blazer and button-down business shirt – and shook his head. "Nah, don't think so. He doesn't look like a criminal to me. And he's leaving the country anyway." He winked at John.

Comair, a city hopping feeder airline, used mostly small twin-engined propeller-driven aircraft, eliminating the need of jetways to board them, and stepping out of the air-conditioned terminal building on to the tarmac was like stepping into an oven. John took his blazer off and carried it over his arm.

At the aircraft, Liz put one foot on the steps, then stopped and looked around her. "I might never forgive you for taking me away from all this, John."

The aircraft's seating configuration was two seats on each side, with a narrow aisle between them. Liz, at five-foot-nothing, had no difficulty walking upright to their seats. John, at six-foot-one had to stoop. Their seats overlooked a wing. Liz took the window seat. She had legroom to spare. John had to put one leg in the aisle and the other one under the seat in front of her.

As they flew over the Florida coastline, a voice from across the aisle said, "You people English?"

John looked over.

The voice belonged to a shaven-headed man in his late twenties/early thirties. He was wearing a clean white T-shirt, faded jeans, and elaborately-tooled cowboy boots. He had a gold stud in his ear and a gold Rolex watch on his wrist. His head reminded John of an ostrich egg he had once seen on a business trip to South Africa.

"Yes, we are," John said. "Is it that obvious?"

"Yeah, kind of. You guys going to Freeport to gamble?"

"No, we're going to live there."

"Jeez! I sure as hell wouldn't want to live there," the egg-head said. "No sirree."

"Oh, and why would that be?" Liz said, leaning forward so she could get a better look at him.

"Because you can't trust anybody. They're all on the take."

"Brilliant!" Liz muttered.

They were flying over the Outer Islands, and they stretched away into the distance. Each island was surrounded by pure white sand, and water which turned from aquamarine to emerald green as the depth increased.

"Look at that," John said, pointing down. "Isn't that beautiful?"

Liz ignored him.

At ninety miles in length, Grand Bahama was the largest of the archipeligo nation's seven hundred islands. Both ends of it were visible as the plane began its initial descent, making it seem much smaller.

The plane made a soft landing and taxied to the airport's little pink and white terminal building, which would have fitted with room to spare on any one of the floors of Orlando International Airport's parking garage.

Three booths were manned in the immigration hall and John headed for the only officer wearing a smile; a large jolly-looking Bahamian woman who seemed intent on enjoying life, despite the job she had been saddled with.

John handed over their passports and immigration forms.

"What's the purpose of your visit?"

"I'm looking for a business to buy into," John said. "I've been trying to find something in Florida, but I haven't been able. I thought I might try my luck here."

"So you're planning to stay awhile."

"Forever if I have anything to do with it," Liz said grimly.

The immigration officer smiled. "Like that, is it?"

"I've told him that if he doesn't find what he's looking for here, I'm going back to England, with, or without him."

"Oh, dear." The immigration officer grinned at John. "Sounds like you're in BIG trouble. You folks bringing capital to the island?"

"It's already here," John said. "It's in an account in Nassau."

"We're always happy to welcome folks with capital."

The immigration officer banged a stamp in each of their passports. "I'm giving you six months. If you need more time, you can get an extension at the immigration office in town. Welcome to the Bahamas."

"It's a damn sight easier getting in here than it is getting into the US," John remarked, as they headed for the baggage-claim area.

"And what does that tell you?" Liz said.

The baggage-claim area was housed in a rusty, corrugated-iron building. A Turkish bath would have been less hot and humid.

Liz caught John looking at the way her hair was sticking to her face. She glared at him. "Don't say a word."

John called a porter with a trolley. They collected their luggage and breezed through customs.

The taxis lined up around the semi-circle forming the airport's drop-off and collection point were American cars circa the 1960s, the era of the Fonz and Happy Days from American TV way back when.

Their porter led them to an ancient Chevrolet, which seemed to have more rust than bodywork. It was leaning to the left, as if the suspension on the left-hand side had collapsed. The driver was huge. Not fat, just huge, and he handled their heavy suitcases as if they were filled with air. When he slammed the boot lid, a pile of rust dropped on to the road. John watched nervously as he slung their golf bags on the roof rack and lashed them down. "Are you sure they're safe up there?" he said.

"Ain't lost nuthin' yet," the big man said.

John had always used a rate of a dollar-a-bag, plus ten percent, when tipping porters in America and he was astounded when the porter asked him for twenty dollars. They had four suitcases and two golf bags, which, according to John's reckoning, amounted to less than ten dollars, but he couldn't be bothered standing around arguing with the man, so he gave him a twenty-dollar bill and climbed into the vehicle.

It was like sitting in an oven.

Liz was sitting on the back seat fanning herself with a Wall Street Journal she had found on the rear seat.

When the driver climbed into the vehicle, the suspension creaked and groaned. He slammed the door. He had to slam it again to get it to close properly.

"Where to?"

John gave him the address. "And would you mind putting the air-conditioning on. It's hard to breathe in here."

"Air con ain't worked in years," the driver said, lurching away from the curb. "Leave the windows down and you'll be fine."

Sitting on a seat that had long since given up trying to support the weight of a human being, John tried to engage Liz in conversation. She ignored him, so he tried the driver. "So what's happening on the island then?"

The driver shrugged his massive shoulders. "Crime's on the increase."

"What sort of crimes?" Liz said.

"Burglaries, rapes, that kind of thing. And some white folks got held up by a gang with Uzis in the Straw Market."

"What are Uzis?" Liz enquired.

John pretended he hadn't heard. Which wasn't difficult considering the gale blowing through the windows.

"They sub-machine guns, ma'am," the driver said.

"Are you listening, John?" Liz said.

They had made a visit to the island once before, to check it out. Liz hadn't been happy about it then, but John had talked her into it, and he had rented a luxury duplex apartment in a gated development backing on to a beach on the south side of the island. The development was relatively new and only three blocks had been built so far. Only a handful of the apartments had been sold, so they were not expecting to have many neighbours.

When the taxi ground to a halt in front of their building, John noticed that the meter had not been turned on. "Why didn't you turn the meter on?" he asked the driver.

"Meter ain't worked in years," came the laconic reply.

They all climbed out of the vehicle.

"So what's the damage?" John asked.

"Seventy-five dollars."

John couldn't believe his ears. "*Seventy-five dollars*? For a twenty-minute ride? You've got to be kidding."

"No, man, I never kid about money."

The driver dumped their golf bags and suitcases on the pavement, took the money, got back in the vehicle and drove off in a cloud of smoke.

John stood there fuming.

"Don't say I didn't tell you," Liz said. "Welcome to the Bahamas."

"Very funny," John snorted.

"Don't say you weren't warned."

John rounded on her, his eyes blazing. "And what the hell am I supposed to do, Liz? Get us back on the next flight back to Florida just because some bald-headed clown on a plane says something? Wait here, I'll get the key."

There was a hotel on the other side of the channel and the sound of children playing in the outdoor pool reassured her. John was taking his time, and she wandered round the back of the building.

Immediately behind the building, was an L-shaped swimming pool with a thatched-roofed bar. There was no one around and Liz walked to the edge of the pool and slipped off her shoes. She dipped her toe in the water, to test the temperature, then she carried her shoes down to the beach, a distance of no more than thirty yards, and stepped into the water. It was warm.

Two people were snorkelling along the side of a rocky causeway forming the entrance to a wide channel, which ran inland past the development.

The apartment comprised the first and second floor of the left-hand end of the building furthest from the channel and access was up a flight of concrete steps. They were about to make a start of carting everything up the steps when a sport fishing boat cruised by in the channel. An attractive young woman in a black bikini sat in the fishing chair on the lower deck, and a middle-aged man in shorts and a sailing cap stood at the controls on the tuna tower above her head. His thick white hair and white beard gave him the appearance of a retired naval officer. They waved and called hi.

John and Liz waved and called hi back.

The kitchen possessed most of the modern conveniences known to mankind, and, in truth, this was one of the reasons Liz had agreed to come; that, and the location. The kitchen led through into a dining area with a marble-topped table and six dining chairs, which then led through into a living area with modern Florida-style furniture. At the far end of the fifty-foot through-room were sliding glass doors leading on to a balcony, which overlooked the beach. On the balcony, which was the width of the living room, was a small dining set comprising a wrought-iron table and four wrought-iron chairs.

There were slatted windows along the long wall of the through room, to allow in sea breezes, and there were ceiling fans to keep the air moving. The apartment was fully air-conditioned.

A staircase from the living area afforded access to the upper floor. This floor contained two double bedrooms, one overlooking the parking area at the front of the building, and the other one, the master bedroom, overlooking the beach. The master bedroom had its own balcony, and its own en-suite bathroom. There was a family bathroom, with bath and walk-in shower, midway between the two bedrooms.

They dumped everything on the living room floor, and Liz made coffee. They carried it out on to the balcony and sat at the wrought-iron table.

A yacht of sixty or seventy feet in length slid down the channel, heading for the ocean. It was running on its engine. The crew spotted them and waved, then got back to their task of unfurling the sails in preparation for their voyage to heaven-knows-where.

Liz had kicked off her shoes and she was sitting with her feet on the balcony rail.

And she was smiling.

The howl of a multi-engine powerboat hurtling down the channel woke John with a start in the early hours of the next morning. He leapt out of bed, fumbled with the lock on the sliding glass door, yanked the door open and leapt out on to the balcony.

There was nothing to see. There was no moon, ergo almost total darkness, and the boat was long gone. It must have been travelling at an enormous speed because the sound of its engines was rapidly receding. The waves it had created were slapping on the rocks forming the causeway.

Chapter 3

Next morning, they were carrying the dishes back into the apartment after breakfast on the balcony when there was a knock on the kitchen door.

It was Rolly Schaerer, their landlord. Knowing they had no car, and would need to stock up on food, he had come to offer them a ride into Freeport. He was a dead ringer for Frank Sinatra, especially about the eyes. He owned and ran the development from a sales office in the gatehouse at the entrance to the development. He lived in the ground-floor apartment immediately below them.

They exchanged pleasantries, and Liz offered coffee. "I was just about to make some."

"Black, no sugar. Thanks." Schaerer walked across the kitchen and sat on a high stool at the breakfast bar. "Happy with your apartment, Liz?"

"Yes, thank you," Liz said. "It's got everything I need, and I love the sea views."

"How long have you been living in the Bahamas?" John asked, perching on the stool beside him.

"Nine years, give or take," Schaerer said. "I was a book publisher and I got tired of the rat race in New York and sold up. I found this piece of land and snapped it up. I'm planning to develop the entire site, all five acres of it."

"Are the apartments selling well?" John asked.

Schaerer rocked his hand in a comme ce, comme ca motion. "Market's a bit slow right now. I've sold five apartments in this block, mostly to overseas investors who want a Bahamas address so they can claim tax-free status, and I have an overseas investor flying in this afternoon with a view to buying the block next door. And I have planning permission for a marina …"

"Off the channel?" John said.

"Yeah, off the channel, and a restaurant. But enough about me, what about you guys? What brought you to the island?"

John took a breath. "Well, to cut a long story short, I sold my business in the UK, and our house, and Liz and I went to live in Orlando. I chose Orlando because I was intending to buy some houses in the Kissimmee area, near Walt Disney World …"

"He was supposed to be retiring," Liz said, getting three mugs out of a cupboard by the sink.

"He's too young to retire," Schaerer said, smiling at Liz. "You said *some* houses, John? How many did you have in mind?"

"I had the cash to buy seven. I was planning to rent six to people coming to Disney, and live in the seventh."

"So why didn't you do it?"

"Because a bank talked me out of it. They reckoned the property boom had peaked, and, like a fool, I listened to them. Then we overstayed on our visas and, rather than go back to the UK, we decided to come here."

"Correction, *you* decided to come here," Liz said, pouring the coffee.

"What kind of visas did you have?"

"B1/B2 business visas."

"Which gave you how long in the country?"

"Six months."

"You could have taken a quick trip out of the country, then gone back in. A quick trip here, for instance. That would have given you another six months. I know people who have done that. In fact, I know one guy who's being doing it for years and is *still* doing it."

"I don't doubt it," John said. "But it's not for me. With my luck, I'd be the one they wouldn't let back into the country. Besides, I hadn't found what I was looking for."

"What *are* you looking for?"

"Why don't we take our coffee on the balcony," Liz said. "It's such a beautiful day out there. It's a shame to waste it sitting in here." She handed them their coffee and they followed her out.

A huge motor-yacht was negotiating its way into the channel. At first it looked like it wouldn't make it, but it made it with room to spare. There was the low hum of conversation and the rattle of crockery from people having breakfast at the hotel across the channel, and the mouth-watering smell of bacon cooking was drifting their way.

They sat down and sipped their coffee.

"So, John, you were about to tell me what you're looking for."

John put his coffee down. "I'm looking for a business to buy into."

"As opposed to starting a new one."

"Yes. I've started several businesses in my time. I thought I'd have a change this time."

"In what field?"

John shrugged. "I can be flexible on that. But probably something in property, or tourism."

"Then how about buying some of my apartments? You could rent them out, which is pretty much what you were planning to do in Florida. I'll cut you a deal if you buy a few of them."

John squeezed Schaerer's forearm. "I appreciate the offer, Rolly, but there's no Walt Disney World here. Disney is what drew me to Orlando, and it's what draws punters from all over the world."

"You could do two-centre holidays; a week in Orlando, and a week here. Lots of travel companies are offering two-centre holidays. We have several great golf courses, deep-sea fishing, wrecks to scuba dive around, sailing, snorkelling, gambling, *and* some great restaurants. Pier One, out by the harbour, is regarded as one of the finest seafood restaurants in the Bahamas, and they put on a fantastic shark-feeding frenzy every night of the week. It draws people from far and wide.

Not to mention we have the same sun as Florida. And Orlando is only an hour away, by air."

John threw back his head and laughed. "Enough already! You're a great salesman, Rolly, but it's not really what I'm after. I'd rather find a business I can involve myself in on a hands-on basis. Something I can work on day to day, something to keep me occupied. If all I had to do was make sure the rents were paid on time, I think it would drive me mad. I bore easily."

"I can vouch for that," Liz said. "He always has to be doing *something*."

Schaerer nodded. "Okay, John. I'll keep my ears to the ground for you."

A speedboat howled down the channel.

Schaerer watched it in disgust. "Idiot!" he exclaimed. "There's a ten mile an hour speed limit on the channel!"

The bow wave the boat was generating was slapping on the rocks and it reminded John of the boat that had woken him in the early hours of that morning. "Speaking of boats, Rolly," he said. "Did you hear that boat in the middle of the night?"

"Sure did. It's hard to sleep through that racket."

"What boat?" Liz said.

"You slept through it," John said. "You were away with the fairies. What do you reckon it was, Rolly?"

Schaerer shrugged. "The usual, I guess. Drug runners."

"*Drug runners?*" Liz cried.

"It's nothing you need concern yourself about, Liz," Schaerer said. "They won't bother you if you don't bother them. The Colombian suppliers use Freeport as a stopping-off point en route to Miami. They run at the dead of night, when there's no moon. Their boats are painted matte black so the Coast Guard helicopter can't see them."

"The way the sound receded, it must have been travelling at a hell of a speed," John said.

"They use Cigarette boats. Some of them have four outboards on them, with upwards of a thousand horsepower on tap. They're so fast that the Coast Guard helicopters can't keep up with them."

"I can see why they run when there's no moon," John said. "The moon would be like shining a torch on them."

"That's exactly right. The only thing that gives them away is the noise they make. But if there's a Coast Guard helicopter in the vicinity, they shut down and drift until the guys in the helicopter call it a day."

"What do they do with their boats during the day?" Liz asked. "Do they hide them away?"

Schaerer shook his head. "No they don't hide them away. They know the authorities can only pick them up if they catch them with drugs on board, and you'll see them tied up at Port Lucaya, just up the channel, with mechanics working on them, in full view. And you see them coming down the channel to make high-speed test runs across the bay in broad daylight."

"Cheeky devils," John said.

Schaerer checked his watch. "Guys, my investor's plane is due in at two, and I told him I'd pick him up at the airport. So if we're going to do that food shopping, we'd better make a start."

Chapter 4

"So what are we going to do today?" Liz asked, the next morning.

The roar of a long sleek powerboat thundering down the channel drowned out John's reply.

A man and a woman fishing off the end of the causeway looked up in alarm and scrambled to the top of the rocks. The bow wave missed them, but the spray from the wave hitting the rocks drenched them.

The boat was powered by four huge outboard engines and it was the length of a London bus. It was painted matte black. Two black youths stood in the open cockpit.

One of the boat's engines seemed to be misfiring, and it made several high-speed passes along the shoreline, before turning and heading back towards the channel. It slowed to enter the channel, and the driver raised a hand to the couple on the rocks.

"Well, they might be drug runners," John said, getting back to his breakfast, "but at least they seem to have some manners."

They were stuck out here without a car, and, when John finished his breakfast, he phoned a taxi firm and had them drive him to the airport so he could rent one.

On checking with the various car rental companies, he discovered that there was a big travel and tourism convention going on in Freeport and that all the rental cars had been taken. He was given the option of waiting until the convention ended, which was three days from now, or taking a fifteen year old-Honda Civic which was normally used as a runabout. It was a no-brainer. He needed a car and he took it. It was filthy, inside and out, and he insisted on them cleaning it before he took it.

Liz had said she thought she would enjoy fishing off the rocks, and he drove into Freeport to look for a shop selling fishing gear. He found one on the outskirts of town. Having only ever fished a couple of times in his life, he had no real idea of what he was looking for, and the shop seemed to cater more for serious deep-sea fishermen than for people looking to catch a few fish off the end of a causeway. He wandered around having no idea what he was looking for until the owner of the shop finished serving a group of Americans who were over for a tuna-fishing trip and took pity on him and came over and asked if he could help.

John walked out of the shop with two slim fibreglass rods about five feet long, two reels, and a tackle box containing an assortment of hooks of different sizes, lead weights, a sharp knife, and a pair of rubber-handled pliers. He had also bought two packets of frozen squid, for bait, and a book entitled *Fishing in the Waters of the Bahamas*.

When he got back to the apartment, he spotted Liz lying on a towel on the beach in her bathing costume. He went down to join her.

"Did you get a car?" she said, sitting up and shading her eyes against the sun.

"Yes, I got one," he said. "It's an old banger, because there's a convention in town and all the cars were out, but at least we'll be mobile. But guess what else I got."

"Tickets to a Buckingham Palace garden party?"

"No, silly. I got a couple of fishing rods."

Her eyes lit up. "You *did*? That's brilliant, John. Well done you."

The rocks looked relatively small and evenly spaced from the apartment, but close up it was a different story altogether. They were much bigger than they looked, and they had been laid in a haphazard way, as if a giant had casually tossed them there. As a result, getting to the end of the causeway required considerable care and concentration, as one slip could have resulted in serious abrasions, or even broken bones. They helped each other along, and took their time.

John was carrying the rods, and the tackle box. He had already fastened the reels to the rods. The bait was in the tackle box.

Liz was carrying a plastic bucket she had found in a cupboard in the kitchen, to carry home whatever they caught, and the book on fishing in Bahamian waters John had bought. She had spent the afternoon lying on the sofa reading the book, and she had discovered that some species of fish found in Bahamian waters were poisonous. She had brought the book along so they could identify what they caught, before deciding which to keep, and which to throw back.

They set up shop on the top of a large and relatively flat rock at the far end of the causeway.

John bent down and opened the tackle box, then squatted on his haunches and selected two hooks of what he thought would be about the right size. He tied a hook on the end of each line. Then he selected what he thought would be the right size of lead weight, and, using the pliers provided, crushed them on to the lines. He had no idea what he was doing, but he figured that four weights on each line should be enough to enable them to make casts of satisfactory distances. He then opened the packet of squid. He had brought one packet, leaving the other packet in the freezer for another time. The squid had defrosted, and he was able to cut it without difficulty. He cut it into half-inch cubes, and attached a piece to each hook.

While he was doing this, Liz spent her time sitting on a neighbouring rock studying the book.

When he was done, and the rods were ready for use, John handed Liz a rod and hopped to another rock. "So we don't get our lines crossed," he said.

They agreed that he would fish to the left, and she would fish to the right.

Liz cast first. At least she tried. Her hook snagged on a rock behind her.

John clambered over the rocks and unhooked it for her. "Try casting it in the water next time," he said, grinning.

She stuck her tongue out at him. "Smarty pants. Let's see how good you are."

Initially, he wasn't much better.

They both improved.

With so many fish in the water, it would have been difficult *not* to catch some, and it wasn't long before they had caught more fish than they could eat.

Until they had begun to recognise the species they were catching, Liz had identified each fish, and most of the fish were now standing on their heads in the bucket. Some tails were still twitching. They were mostly jacks, grunts, and snapper, all of which the book said made for excellent eating.

Liz had hooked one fish that had set her heart racing. In fact, it had put up such a struggle that, exhausted, she had eventually handed her rod to John.

When John finally got the fish close enough to the rocks that they could see it, it was over two feet long, it was about the thickness of a strong man's forearm, and it had rows of what appeared to be razor-sharp teeth.

He lifted it out of the water, with the rod bent double, while Liz checked what it was with the book.

"Oh my God," she said, "it's a barracuda."

"What does it say about them?" John said, anxious to do something with the fish. It was heavy and he was afraid the rod, which was bent in an inverted u-shape, would break.

Liz squinted at the book. "It says, and I quote: 'Treat barracuda with the greatest respect. They can grow up to five feet in length, and the larger ones should be released by cutting the line. The smaller fish should be held in a gloved-hand while removing the hook with a pair of pliers. Eating barracuda can result in cigureta poisoning.'"

They had no glove, so John wrapped his handkerchief round the fish, and, keeping his other hand well away from its teeth, he gripped the hook with the business end of the pliers and, twisting and turning it as gently as possible, so as not to cause the fish any more suffering than was absolutely necessary, he pulled the hook out. The fish, which had lain perfectly still in his hand, glared at him malevolently. He tossed it back in the water. It sank below the surface, then took off as if it had been fired from a rifle.

He shivered as he watched it go. He was glad to see the back of it.

Making their way back over the rocks was even more difficult than it had been before, because John now had a bucketful of fish to contend with, and it was heavy. But they helped each other along and took their time, and made it back without mishap.

Back at the apartment, John poured the fish into the kitchen sink, and rinsed out the bucket. He then got a bottle of Chardonnay from the fridge and poured them each a glass, sipping his as he topped, tailed, and filleted the fish.

He had never filleted a fish in his life, but he was not one to shy away from a challenge, and, using the sharpest knife he could find in the knife drawer, he made what he thought was a reasonably respectable effort.

Liz then breaded the fillets and fried them in vegetable oil. She served them with new potatoes and a green salad on the side and they ate on the balcony, washing their meal down with a bottle of chilled Sancerre.

When they had finished eating, John sat back in his chair and patted his belly. "Well," he said, utterly satisfied, "fish doesn't come any fresher than *that*."

Chapter 5

Three evenings later, they had had dinner and were putting their dishes in the dishwasher and thinking of having an early night, when there was a knock on the kitchen door.

"Who on earth can that be at this time of night?" Liz said, looking at her watch.

"Only one way to find out," John said. He opened the door.

It was Rolly Schaerer, and he had with him a tall dark-haired woman in a red dress. "Sorry about the lateness of the hour, John," he said, "but, Sybille, here has a business proposition I thought you should hear about. And I figured sooner rather than later, in case somebody else snaps it up."

"Then you'd better come in," John said. He estimated Sybille to be in her early to mid-forties. She was an attractive woman, handsome rather than beautiful, and there was something overtly sexual about the way she moved. She was wearing a dress that looked as if it had seen better days, and her jewellery was costume, and not very good costume at that.

Over drinks on the balcony, Sybille, whose full name was Sybille Johanssen, told them she was French Canadian, divorced, with a son of twenty-four, who lived in Canada, and that she had been living on the island for just over seven years. "That's it, really. Me, in a nutshell."

"And if you believe that, you'll believe anything," Schaerer said. "What she failed to tell you is that she's a qualified scuba-diving instructor and she takes people out to dive sites. She's quite a celebrity in these parts."

"So, we have a celebrity in our midst," John said. He gave Sybille a little bow. "We're honoured, Sybille."

"Thank you, John," Sybille said.

"I quite like the idea of learning to scuba-dive," John said. "Perhaps you would give me a lesson, or two."

"I'd be happy too," Sybille said. "Rolly has my number."

"So tell me something about this business proposition of yours," John said.

Sybille explained that for the last five years she had been managing a property on the north side of the island, and that the owner of the property, an elderly man now suffering from dementia, had just told her that if she paid him $4,000 a month, she could do as she wished with the property. She explained that because of his illness he had let the property slide and had had to resort to taking in terminally-ill cancer patients from the hospital to generate income. She said that the new oncology wing at the hospital was due to open in three month's time, and that the cancer patients would then be gone, and the income would dry up. She said that the owner then planned to leave and move to Miami, where he would get better treatment for his condition, and where his daughter lived.

Sybille went on to say that she had never in her life had an opportunity like this, and that she had no intention of missing out on it. She said she had come up with the idea of finding an investor to renovate the property, and to then put the property on the market. She described the property as thirty-six one-bedroom apartments arranged in three two-storey buildings around a swimming pool. She said that the property included two acres of tropical gardens, and that it backed on to a beach that overlooked the Atlantic Ocean.

Liz had been building a picture of the property in her mind as Sybille was describing it, and when Sybille had finished talking, she said, "It sounds lovely, Sybille."

Sybille smiled at her, pleased. "It will be when it's been renovated, Liz," she said. "It will be beautiful. I can see it now."

What Sybille had described was ticking John's boxes. He would have preferred to be involved in something that went on into the future; a business he could build up, but this was not to be sneezed at. "Have you discussed your plans with the owner of the property?" he asked.

"Yes, I have. And he's fine with them. By the way, he's living on the property, and so am I."

"Assuming this went ahead, Sybille, would he still own the property while you were paying him the $4,000 a month?"

"Yes, he would. He would own the property until the last apartment had been bought, and paid for. And by the way, I should add that he wants $5,000 on the sale of each apartment. He regards this as his pension fund."

"How long do you think the renovations would take?"

"Rolly knows the property and he thought six to nine months," Sybille said. "We should be in and out within a year."

"I need a pencil and paper," John said.

"In the kitchen," Liz said. "I'll get them for you."

She came back with a legal pad and pencil.

John started making notes. "A year, you say, Sybille?"

"About that, John, yes."

"Then that would be twelve monthly payments of $4,000 each, meaning $48,000. On top of that there's the $5,000 per apartment the owner wants, and thirty-six apartments at $5,000 a pop amounts to $180,000. What do you think the renovations would cost?"

"Say two fifty grand."

"Okay." John added this to the list. "Have I missed anything?"

Sybille shook her head. "I don't think so."

"So, the total cost, assuming it *does* only take a year to renovate and sell the apartments, amounts to $478,000."

"You're *kidding*," Sybille said, frowning. "I didn't think it would be that much."

John got back to his sums. "And, assuming the apartments sold for $30,000, we would be looking at …let's see…a profit of $502,000. And, split two ways, that would give each participant $250,000. That's not bad for a year's work. What do you say, Rolly?"

"I'd say that was pretty good, John. You would get a one hundred percent return on your investment, and you, Sybille, would get a cool two hundred and fifty grand, with no money down. I'd say that was a hell of a deal, for both of you."

"And I would agree with you," John said. "Well, this looks interesting. Very interesting, actually."

"Not to me, it doesn't," Sybille said. "I expected to get a lot more out of it than that, and if you think I'm coming up with a deal like this and only getting a measly two hundred and fifty grand out of it, you can think again.

"All right, Sybille," John said, "then let's know how much you're looking for."

"I want four hundred grand. At the *very least*."

John thought for a moment or two and then said: "Well, as I see it, the only way you could get that much out of it would be to either reduce the cost of the renovations, or get a higher price for the apartments."

"There is another way," Sybille said. "We could split the profit sixty-forty, in my favour. What would that give me?"

Liz looked ready to blow a gasket. "What would that give *you*?" she demanded. "You selfish bitch. Why should you get more than John?"

In all the years John had known Liz, he had never heard her speak to anyone like that. But she had a point.

Sybille looked at Liz in disbelief. "What did you just say to me?"

"I asked you why you should get more than John. You should get the same. Asking for sixty percent is being just plain greedy."

"I meant you calling me a bitch," Sybille said. "No one calls *me* a bitch and gets away with it."

"Then perhaps it's time someone did."

Sybille's eyes narrowed. "Were you aware that I practise witchcraft?"

"No, I wasn't," Liz said scornfully. "Well, bully for you."

Schaerer got to his feet. "Come on, Sybille. It's time to go."

"Sit down," Sybille said, "I'm not finished. I practise the kind of witchcraft, *Liz*, where effigies of people get buried in the seabed. "

"And what's that supposed to achieve?" Liz snorted. "Apart from an effigy getting a watery grave."

"You may scoff, Liz, but you really should take it seriously. What it achieves is it commits the soul to eternal damnation."

Schaerer didn't know where to put himself. "Thanks, guys. It's been really ..."

But Liz hadn't finished. "Will you put a spell on John if he doesn't take you up on your offer?"

Sybille smiled at her. "John's much too nice a guy to put a spell on, but you, Liz? I might be tempted to put a spell on you."

Schaerer took her arm. "Sybille, that's enough! We're leaving."

Sybille shook John's hand, and, to annoy Liz, she held on to it. "Thank you, John. I really enjoyed the evening. And do think about the deal. We probably *could* do fifty-fifty."

"Sybille," Liz said, "if I have anything to do with it, you'll be lucky to get *five* percent. And holding on to my husband's hand doesn't impress me, because I trust him."

Schaerer took John's arm. "John, I'm really ..."

"Don't worry about it, Rolly," John said. "I'll see you out."

Two minutes later, the sound of a door slamming and glass breaking shattered the peace of the evening.

"I wonder what stone he found her under," Liz said.

Chapter 6

Six weeks after they had arrived on the island, John got a phone call from George Humphries, the forwarding agent who was arranging the shipment of his Grand Cherokee and their personal effects from Florida. He had called to say that everything had arrived and that a customs officer would be inspecting them at two o'clock that afternoon. "And if you want to save yourself some import duty," Humphries said, "you might want to be there. And bring some cash, as well as your cheque book."

From the directions Humphries had given him, John found the bonded warehouse of Bahamas Customs and Excise without difficulty.

It was a corrugated iron building secured by a ten-foot chain-link fence, topped with evil-looking razor wire. It was located a couple of hundred yards from the airport terminal building.

John turned in the rental car at the terminal, and walked back.

When he walked into the Customs building, he recognised the forwarding agent immediately. It was the man who had waved from the boat on the channel the day they had moved into the apartment. They had spoken a number of times over the phone, and had struck up a friendship. He was talking with a uniformed black customs officer. They were standing by his Grand Cherokee and seemed to be having a heated discussion about it.

Humphries heard his footsteps. "Well, hi there," he boomed. He broke off his conversation with the customs officer, and strode over.

"I hadn't realised that was you on the boat, George," John said. He put out his hand. "Nice to finally put a face to a voice."

Humphries pumped his hand vigorously. "Sure is. How are you guys settling in?"

"Just fine, thanks."

"Great. We must get together."

The customs officer was giving the Grand Cherokee a serious once-over.

"He's disputing the value," Humphries said. "He says it looks new. I've told him it's a year-and-a-half old, and it looks new because you've looked after it. Do you have the original invoice?"

The vehicle was eight months old. John had bought it new a few days after they had landed in Florida.

"Didn't I send it to you?"

"I don't think so. No matter. I can deal with this."

John followed him to the vehicle.

"The original invoice seems to have gone walkabout, Harold. Are you prepared to take Mr McLaren's word for its value? I can vouch for his honesty."

Harold shook his head. "You know I can't do that, George. But let's see what else he's got." He tapped a small carton. It was marked FRAGILE. "What's in this?"

Humphries checked the reference number of the carton against the paperwork on his clipboard. "A TV set," he said.

"What size screen does it have?"

Humphries checked his paperwork again.

John knew the TV was listed as having a thirty-eight inch screen.

"Twenty-eight inches."

John wasn't about to play piggy-in-the-middle between these two. He kept his mouth shut.

"It seems a big carton for a twenty-eight inch set," Harold said.

"You know what wasteful bastards us Americans are, Harold. We over-package everything."

"Is it a new set?"

John had bought the TV on the same day he had bought the Jeep. But he was getting into the swing of things here, and, well, eight months couldn't possibly be regarded as new, could it?

"No, it's used," he said.

Harold tapped a cardboard box about fifteen inches high. "What's in here?" It was marked: GLASS – HANDLE WITH CARE.

Humphries consulted his paperwork. "That one's assorted alcoholic drinks, Horace. I guess that's English for booze." He grinned at John.

John grinned back, sharing the joke. "It is," he said. "It's wines, and spirits."

"Open it," Harold said.

Humphries opened it.

Harold bent over and looked in the box. He removed the screwed-up newspaper John had put between the bottles to prevent breakage, and took a look at what the box contained. Clinking the bottles as he moved them around, his eyes lit up when he spotted an unopened bottle of John's favourite scotch, a ten-year-old Macallan single malt. He took it out and stood it by the box. He rummaged around again, and took out an unopened bottle of Finlandia vodka. He then withdrew two bottles of a vintage chateau-bottled claret. Each bottle had probably cost more than Harold made in a month, and John had been saving them for a special occasion.

"Okay," Harold said, standing up straight again. "You can close it up."

Humphries winked at John, and closed the box.

"What's in these?"

These referred to three cartons, which were about five feet tall. They contained clothes, on hangers. They were marked: THIS WAY UP.

"Clothes," John said. "Mostly my wife's."

Harold tapped one of them. "Open this one."

Humphries opened the carton.

As Harold rummaged through Liz's clothes, Humphries drew John to one side. "How much cash did you bring with you?"

"I have about four hundred dollars in my wallet."

"Give me two-fifty."

John got his wallet out of the back pocket of his shorts and counted out twelve twenties, and a ten. He handed the money to Humphries, who palmed it.

"Watch and learn," Humphries said. "We all set, Harold?"

"We're all set, George."

"So what's the damage?" As he asked the question, Humphries slipped the money into Harold's hand. It slid into the Bahamian's pocket with the ease of water running over pebbles in a stream.

"Since it's all for personal use, Mr McLaren, I'll only charge you import duty on the vehicle."

Before John had a chance to respond, Humphries said, "Which means sixty percent on twenty-two thousand dollars. Right, Harold?"

The vehicle was top-of-the-range and he had paid thirty-three thousand dollars for it. John had never been one to throw money around, but he had to force himself to not feel guilty about what was going on here. It was so blatant. And he could see that Harold knew exactly what was going on.

He was giving the forwarding agent a long hard look, which John interpreted to read: One day, my friend, you will try this once too often.

"Very well," Harold said. "Sixty percent on twenty-two thousand dollars, which amounts to thirteen thousand two hundred dollars."

John wrote out a cheque and handed it to him.

While he was doing this, Humphries went to find a cardboard box.

Harold wrote out a receipt, and handed it to John.

Humphries came back with a cardboard box into which he put the bottles. He handed the box to Harold. "Pleasure doing business with you, Harold," he said.

"You too, George," Harold said. He walked away with the box under his arm, the bottles clinking expensively.

"He'll share the booze with his colleagues," Humphries told John. "As to the cash, it's every man for himself. Come on, let's go to my office and get your paperwork sorted, then we can get you on your way."

The forwarding agent's office was a wood-panelled room about fourteen feet square. His desk was leather-topped and he had a matching green leather Captain's chair. There were two matching green leather visitors' chairs in front of his desk, and a small table with four chairs for meeting purposes to one side. There was a credenza with a computer on it behind his desk. On the wall behind his desk, was a stuffed blue marlin in a glass case, and on his desk, in pride of place, was a deep-sea diver's helmet.

A certificate on another wall identified him as head of BASRA, an acronym for Bahamas Air And Sea Rescue, and another certificate identified him as Commodore of the West Bahamas Powerboat Club.

"You ever had a boat, John?" Humphries said, looking over his reading glasses at John.

John wandered over and sat in one the chairs in front of Humphries' desk. "No, I've never had a boat, George. I suppose mostly because I've never lived on water before."

"Well, you're living on water now, and if you're planning to stay on the island, you might want to think about getting one. Apart from it being a lot of fun, and allowing you to go places, it would open up connections for you. Most of the people who matter on the island have a boat."

"Then I'd better give it some thought."

"If you do decide to get one, let me know and I'll point you in the right direction." Humphries handed John an invoice. "That should take care of it."

John glanced at the bottom line. The figure was what they had agreed over the phone, so he wrote out a cheque.

Humphries handed him the keys to the Jeep. "By the way," he said. "Before I forget, my wife …"

"Was that the woman on the boat, the really attractive one?"

"Yeah, the cute gal on the boat, Jill. At least I think she's cute. Well, she suggested you might want to come to our annual club barbecue."

"That sounds like fun. When is it?"

"Sunday week. You guys doing anything?"

John didn't have to think about what they would be doing a week on Sunday, because he knew what they would be doing. They would be doing exactly what they did every day, which was nothing of any consequence, and the idea of a barbecue and meeting interesting people sounded wonderful. And he knew Liz, who was usually in her element when she was meeting people, Sybille notwithstanding, would be delighted to go.

So he said, "I think I can safely say we have absolutely nothing planned Sunday week, so thank you, George, we'd be delighted to come."

"Great. Jill will be thrilled, and so am I. You'll meet some great people."

Humphries wrote down the directions for him. "It's on a beach. And wear shorts. It's too goddamned hot for anything else." He handed John the directions. "We'll probably start eating around one p.m., so get there around twelve so you'll get to meet some people first. We usually get around fifty attending. Great crowd. You'll like 'em."

"Take it we'll be there," John said. "And, thanks, George. I shall look forward to that."

"Good, now let's get your stuff organised."

Humphries picked up the phone. "Have a couple of the guys load Mr McLaren's stuff in the Jeep and bring me the keys. *What*!? Don't give me that bullshit. I don't give a goddamn how busy you are. Do it, and do it now!" He slammed the phone down. "Goddamn Bahamians. It takes 'em a goddamn week to pick their goddamn noses."

Chapter 7

The next time John and Liz met Sybille, it was quite by chance.

It was a Saturday afternoon, and they had just walked out of the shop of the UNECSO - Underwater Exploration Society building at Port Lucaya, having just bought themselves snorkelling gear.

Sybille was on a dive boat, returning from a dive with a group of lively Americans. As the boat prepared to dock, she spotted John and flashed her eyes and ran her fingers through her hair, flirting with him. Then, for Liz's benefit, she pretended she had only just noticed them and waved gaily.

Liz knew exactly what she was up to and took John's. "Come on," she said. "We're leaving."

John was blissfully unaware of what was going on. "I know you don't like her, Liz," he said, "but there's no need to be rude to her."

Liz sighed and shook her head.

The boat docked and Sybille walked around high-fiving the Americans as they disembarked.

"Fantastic dive, Sybille," one of them said. "See you next time."

"Yeah, great dive, Sybille," another one said.

Sybille waited until everyone had disembarked, then jumped off the boat and sauntered over.

Liz stood there fuming.

"Hi there," Sybille said, grinning.

"Good dive?" John asked.

"Great, thanks." Sybille eyed the UNEXSO bag John was carrying. The tips of two pairs of fins protruded from the bag; pink for Liz, black for him. "Been doing a little shopping?"

"We've been buying snorkelling gear. Not much point living on the water if we don't make use of it."

"You look nice, Liz," Sybille said, looking Liz looking up and down.

Liz was wearing a short-sleeved golf shirt, tailored knee-length shorts, and a straw hat. Not wishing to give Sybille the satisfaction of knowing how furious she was at the way Sybille was sucking up to John, she smiled sweetly. "Why, thank you, Sybille. And may I say that's a very nice bathing costume you're wearing."

Sybille was wearing a black one-piece bathing costume. "Oh, this old thing? I wear this because I can get a wet suit over it."

"Have you found an investor for that property of yours, yet?" John said.

Sybille shook her head. "No, I haven't, John. You wouldn't still be interested, would you?"

"Not at sixty-forty in your favour, I wouldn't."

"What if we went back to the original fifty-fifty? Would you be interested then?"

"Well, at fifty-fifty ..."

Liz told a barefaced lie. "I'm sorry, Sybille, but we have to go. We're meeting some people and we're late already." She dragged John away.

Chapter 8

The day of George Humphries' beach barbecue undoubtedly was, to Bahamians, just another boring day in paradise. There was uninterrupted blue sky as far as the eye could see.

John parked the Grand Cherokee behind two other cars in the shade of a long stand of pine trees separating the road from the beach. Before switching off the engine, he let all the windows down an inch or so to let out the heat, and to let in whatever sea breezes might happen to come their way. Then he and Liz put on the straw hats they had acquired at Port Lucaya the previous day, and wandered down to the beach.

Frank Sinatra's ballad *I Did It My Way* was belting out of huge speakers in the back of an old blue van bearing the name of George Humphries' company.

The group on the beach was perhaps forty strong. Three or four people seemed to be older, and a handful younger, but most of them appeared to be around John and Liz's age. Everyone wore shorts and many were barefoot. What few children there were, were running in and out of trees, playing tag.

A veritable armada of powerboats of all shapes and sizes bobbed gently at anchor thirty to forty yards off the beach. Considering how few cars there were, most of the people had come by boat.

Four trestle tables laden with plates of food wrapped in cling-film had been laid end-to-end in the shade of the trees, and two women were putting out paper plates.

George Humphries was standing in a cloud of smoke at a barbecue grill. He had a wooden-handled fork in one hand and a glass of red wine in the other. He wore a chef's hat and an apron with the body of a naked woman printed on it. He was gyrating to the music. He was cooking hamburgers and the charcoal was hissing and spitting. He raised an arm and yelled, "Hey there! Glad you could make it."

When John introduced him to Liz, Humphries threw his arms round her and wrapped her in a great bear hug.

Liz emerged laughing.

Humphries' wife, Jill, was petite, dark-haired and vivacious. She was also considerably younger than her husband. The top three buttons of her blue denim shirt were open, revealing a tantalising amount of cleavage. She was deeply tanned and John was tempted to ask if she was that colour all over. From her accent, he thought she might be from the Boston area.

Liz and Jill air-kissed each other's cheeks and greeted each other like long-lost sisters.

John shook Jill's hand. Her grip was strong, more like a man's than a woman's. She asked how they were settling in.

"We're getting there," Liz said.

"I'm glad you could make it. We see the same faces year in and year out, and it's good to have new blood on the island. George, why don't you look after Liz, and I'll look after John."

"Sure thing, honey," Humphries said. "Let me find somebody to take over the cooking, then we'll find you a glass of Champagne."

Jill took John's arm and led him to the trestle tables. There were several coolers under the trestle tables and she took the lid off one of them, exposing several bottles of Champagne on ice. She filled a plastic flute and handed it to John.

"Sorry about the plastic," she said. "We don't use glass on the beach in case it gets broken and someone steps on it." She slipped her arm through his and led him off to meet people.

Within forty minutes of getting there, John had met the owner of a golf course, the owner of a hotel/casino complex, a Belgian couple who had introduced a herd of dairy cows to the island – giving people living on the island the opportunity to buy fresh milk for the very first time, and an Englishman who owned the largest jewellery business in the Caribbean and flew his own plane. Most of them were living in the Bahamas for reasons of tax, which served to reinforce John's view that – if he chose to work with Sybille – his idea of offering her apartments on the international market for tax reasons was a sound one.

One individual of particular interest to John was a Canadian property developer by the name of Jack Smith. As Jill introduced them, she mentioned that Smith was the developer responsible for building Port Lucaya. "If anyone knows what's going on property-wise on the island, it's Jack."

At this point, Jill was called away to help with the food and John took the opportunity to have a word with the developer about Sybille's property, without actually mentioning Sybille by name.

"Sounds to me like you're talking about Sybille Johanssen's place," Smith said.

Jill had been right; he did know what he was doing. "I am talking about Sybille's place. And if you were in my position, Jack, what would you do?"

"That would depend on the deal she offered me."

John explained what Sybille had offered him, quoting the fifty-fifty she had mentioned yesterday.

"Will you need to borrow money?"

John shook his head. "No. I have more than enough capital to cover the renovations."

"Then, if I were in your position, I'd go ahead. There are no other deals like that on the island at the moment, that's for sure."

"*Lunch*," someone called.

Smith took his wallet from the back pocket of his shorts and took out a business card. "Let me know if you decide to go ahead. I know a guy who could do the work for you. Someone you could trust."

The food would have put many a fine restaurant to shame. These people clearly demanded the best. Jill announced that Pier One had donated the Alaskan king crab legs and the Australian lobster tails.

Redwood picnic tables were dotted among the trees and John and Liz found themselves a table and sat down to eat.

Jill walked over with a bottle of Champagne.

"My, what service," Liz said.

"I don't do this for everyone," Jill said. She topped up their glasses and moved on to the next table.

"She's lovely," Liz said. "I do like her."

"Yes, she's a sweetie," John said. "I like George too."

"So do I. He's good fun. I can see us becoming friends with them." Liz picked up a piece of Alaskan king crab leg. "Have you met anybody interesting?"

"I have, as it happens," John said, peeling an Atlantic king prawn. "The guy who built Port Lucaya."

"What did he have to say?"

John took a sip of Champagne. "You might not want to know about it."

"By which, I take it, it had something to do with Sybille and that property of hers."

"Correct."

"And, purely out of curiosity, what did he say?"

"He said that if he were in my position, he would go ahead with it. He said there isn't another deal like it on the island. He even said he could put me in touch with someone to handle the renovations."

"John, I can't stand the woman. There's no way I could work with her."

"You wouldn't have to work with her, Liz. All you would need to do is countersign the cheques. I would do the rest."

"John, please. Can we talk about this some other time? I don't want to spoil an otherwise perfect day by having an argument with you."

Later that afternoon, the roar of high-powered boat engines destroyed the peace as people started to leave. John and Liz stayed behind to help the Humphries clear up.

Liz helped Jill gather up the used paper plates, plastic glasses and plastic cutlery, and dump them in plastic bin liners, which they then loaded into the back of the van. Jill wrapped the surplus food in cling film to give to a nursing home in Freeport that she and her husband supported.

John dug a hole in the sand and helped Humphries bury the hot ash from the barbecue. Then he helped him collapse the trestle tables and load them into the van.

"OK, we're all set," Humphries, said, closing the van doors. "Thanks for your help, guys."

"I'll call you during the week, Liz," Jill said, giving Liz a hug.

"And we'll work out a convenient date to take you to Pier One," Humphries said.

As they climbed into the stifling interior of the Grand Cherokee, John said, "Well, how do you feel about living in the Bahamas now?"

"I love it," Liz said. "But I still don't want you to have anything to do with Sybille."

Chapter 9

A week later, Liz had just got back from a visit to the Straw Market in Freeport with Jill when Rolly Schaerer phoned.

"You guys doing anything tonight?"

"I don't think so," Liz said. "Nothing we can't change, at any rate. What did you have in mind?"

"I'm going fishing on the reef and I wondered if you guys would like to join me."

"I'd need to check with John, but it sounds good to me."

"The thing is, Liz, that ... Sybille will be with me."

"In that case, we'll pass. But thank you for the invitation."

"Actually, Liz, I was hoping you would come *because* Sybille will be with me.

"I don't think so, Rolly. But thank you, anyway."

"Liz, would it help if I gave you some background about Sybille? There are reasons she is as she is."

"I'm sure there are, but I'm not sure I'm all that interested."

"Liz, indulge me, please. You might feel differently about her if you knew a little of her background."

Liz sighed. "All right, Rolly, if you must. But I can't see it making any difference." Liz carried the phone out on to the balcony and sat down at the table.

John was snorkelling by the rocks of the causeway.

Schaerer explained how Sybille had been born in a mining town in Canada to a father who left home when she was six and a mother who, when her father left home, turned to drink, then to heroin, then to prostitution to feed her heroin habit; and about how the walls were paper-thin and Sybille had to listen to everything men were doing to her mother; and about how two of the men raped Sybille when she was thirteen years of age and her mother had thrown her out, calling her a liability; and about how she moved in with a man who made her pregnant almost immediately and then left her when the baby was born.

"She was seventeen at the time. I just wanted to make the point that she's had a rough time of it, and I thought it might help if you knew what she had been through."

"I'm not sure that having sympathy for what she has been through will make any difference to how I feel about her, Rolly, but she certainly didn't deserve that, and thank you for telling me."

"Liz, I'm seeing a lot of Sybille. We are in a relationship, and I thought it would be nice if we could all be friends. She's not all bad. She actually has some good points when you get to know her."

John was floating on his back waving to her. She waved back to him.

"All right, Rolly, we will come tonight, and we'll see how it works out. What time do you want us?"

"Around six. I'll pick you up."

When Schaerer picked them up that evening, Sybille was in the car with him. She nodded to Liz. "Liz."

Liz nodded back. "Sybille."

They drove to a bungalow backing on to a canal. Schaerer parked in the drive and switched off the engine. He was behaving as if he owned the place and Liz asked him if the people living there minded him parking in their drive.

Schaerer grinned. "No, they don't mind, mostly because I own the place. But they're away at the moment anyway."

He took a cooler from the boot of his car and they followed him round the bungalow to the rear garden.

A large two-masted schooner was tied to a dock at the foot of the garden. An open wooden boat with a small outboard motor was tied to the dock behind it.

"Your yacht too, I suppose," John said.

"Yup."

"And the boat?"

"That too."

"She's a beauty," Liz said, gazing wide-eyed at the yacht. "Can we have a look at her?"

"Of course you can."

They followed him down the garden and stepped on to the dock. He put the cooler in the open boat. John followed suit, putting their rods and tackle box in the boat.

"How much of a crew do you need to sail her?" John asked.

"Who said anything about crew?" Schaerer said, a twinkle in his eye.

"Do you mean you sailed her here yourself?" Liz said, incredulous.

"Sure do."

"You're *kidding!*" John stood there open-mouthed.

"Nope. I sailed her here from New York, I've sailed her to Bermuda, and I've raced her in the Bahamas Americas Cup race every year for the past five years. All single-handed."

"Is there no end to your talents?" John said.

Schaerer grinned. "You'd better ask Sybille."

Sybille smirked. "I'm saying nothing."

"She's lovely, Rolly," Liz said. She walked the length of the dock, admiring the vessel. "I'd love to have a sail in her sometime."

"Then how about you and John joining me in a sail to the West End for this year's Bahamas Americas Cup? It only takes a couple of hours to get there. I'm not sailing in the race, but we can sail out one day, spend the night on the boat, and sail back the next day. Don't expect to get any sleep, because they party all night. But I guarantee you'll have fun. They're a great bunch of people."

"And what about me?" Sybille said, pouting. "Aren't you going to invite me? I *am* supposed to be your girlfriend."

"Only if you promise to behave," Schaerer said. "I don't want a repeat of the last time I took you sailing."

"God! It's like being back at school," Sybille said. "All right, I'll behave. Now are you going to invite me?"

"Okay with you if Sybille comes along, Liz?"

Liz shrugged. "It's your boat. You can invite whoever you like."

"Well thanks for the vote of confidence," Sybille sniffed.

Schaerer walked back up the garden and opened the door at the back of a single garage. He stepped inside and came out with two rods that made the rods John had bought look like children's toys, and a battered tackle box. He laid them on the dock, and then went back. This time he came out of the garage with a large plastic bucket, of the kind that plasterers use, and four buoyancy aids. "And anyone who refuses to wear one, isn't coming," he warned. "Now we need some bait."

"I brought some squid," John ventured.

"I mean *real* bait."

They sat on the lawn while Schaerer fished for bait, and Liz looked away when he cut off the heads of the fish he had caught without killing them first. He put the bodies in the bucket and tossed the heads back in the canal. Finally he said, "Okay, let's go catch some fish."

To balance the boat, and because Liz had the shortest legs, Schaerer had her sit in the bow. He put John and Sybille in the middle. He untied the bowline then stepped into the boat and sat himself down on the seat at the stern. He pulled the cord to fire up the motor. It fired on the third pull, filling the air with the oily smell of two-stroke mix. He untied the stern line and pushed the boat away from the dock.

Every hundred yards or so along the canal there were 10 mph speed limit signs. Less frequently, there were signs reminding boat owners that they were responsible for any damage their bow wave caused.

They puttered on toward the ocean, the little motor leaving a cloud of smoke behind them.

They were literally yards from entering the ocean when they passed a pod of dolphins in a fenced-off inlet to one side of the canal. A wooden building bore the sign: DIVE WITH THE DOLPHINS.

"Ah, I've been wondering where they kept them," John said.

"Where did you think they kept them?" Sybille said. "Tied to a rock on the seabed?" When no one responded to her joke, Sybille threw up her hands in despair. "God, can't someone make a joke? What's wrong with you people?"

Schaerer opened the throttle.

"How far out do we have to go?" John said, almost having to shout to make himself heard above the scream of the little engine.

"The reef's about half a mile out, John," Sybille bawled. "We'll be there in a few minutes."

Their shoulders and thighs were touching: of necessity for John, because of the cramped conditions in the boat, but not so for Sybille, who was taking full advantage of the cramped conditions and enjoying every minute of the close personal contact with John, especially since Liz was facing the other way.

Schaerer finally announced that they had reached the reef, and the respite from the racket, when he shut down the motor, was bliss. The only sounds now were the lapping of the water on the hull, and the cawing of a pair of seagulls overhead,

Schaerer tossed out the anchor. The water must have been deep: it took a lot of rope.

Liz swivelled round to face John. "You okay?" she mouthed.

John suffered from seasickness and it was taking all his willpower not to throw up. He shook his head. "Not really."

"First things first," Schaerer said. He opened the cooler and handed John a can of Budweiser Light.

John had never been a fan of American beer, he found it bland and gaseous, but he took it hoping it might settle his stomach. He drank a third of it in one swallow, and it did seem to help.

Schaerer took the headless body of a plump red snapper from the bucket and cut it into pieces for the others to use as bait. He was going after the big stuff, using lead weights the size of golf balls, hooks you could hang a small pig from, and bait that would have provided a meal for a medium-sized adult. And, while the others were fishing from a seated position, he was standing in the middle of the boat with his legs apart, to balance himself against the swell of the ocean, and casting into the distance. The boat was rocking perilously.

Sybille let him get away with it for while, then she lost her cool. "For God's sake, Rolly, *sit down*! You're going to have us all in the water."

Schaerer sat. He knew better than to disobey Sybille.

Sybille hauled out a fish that looked like a football with spikes. It had saucer-shaped eyes and a mouth that pouted like that of a child that has just been chastized.

Schaerer identified it as a porcupine fish.

"Reminds me of you in a strop," Sybille said, to laughter from all.

John hooked something that felt like a dead weight; in fact, at first, he thought his hook had snagged on the reef. But then he felt movement in the line. His rod bent and quivered as he reeled it in. When it finally broke surface, John found himself looking at an enormous green head with a huge mouth and rows of teeth. It was a moray eel. He had seen pictures of it in the book. The book said they hid in crevices in rocks and reefs, waiting for their prey to swim by.

Schaerer reacted immediately. "Don't touch it, John! It'll take your hand off " He snatched up the knife he had been using to cut bait, and slashed John's line.

The loathsome creature splashed back into the water and slowly sank back into the depths.

Schaerer hooked a fish that raced off with his line. The excitement turned to panic when he ran out of line and the fish started towing the boat. The anchor held and the line snapped. Schaerer, who had been standing up, ended up on his backside in the well of the boat. "Shit!" he muttered, furious with himself for losing the fish.

"Shit nothing," Sybille said. "We might have ended up in Miami."

That broke the ice. They all ended up in fits of laughter.

And Schaerer landed a grouper that was bigger than him. He killed it with a cosh-like object he kept in his tackle box, and, because it was too big and heavy for them to get in the boat, he tied it to the side of the boat, and they towed it back to the bungalow, , where John helped him get it on to the dock.

Schaerer then went into the garage and came out with a serrated-edge knife about eighteen inches long. When John realized what Schaerer was going to do with the knife, he was glad Schaerer was on his side, and the women beat a hasty retreat, because Schaerer sawed off the head of the huge fish, and kicked it in the canal.

John stood and watched the head get smaller as it was attacked by swarms of fish. It was like watching piranha at work. "No wastage there," he said.

"Nature at work," Schaerer said. He sawed the grouper into chunks, which John helped him carry into the garage, where there was a large freezer which was already a third full of frozen fish.

They drove back to the apartment and John organised drinks while Schaerer, who clearly had considerably more experience at preparing fish than he had, topped and tailed the fish, and then expertly filleted them. Or, to use his parlance, *fillayed* them.

Liz grilled the fillets and served them with boiled potatoes and peas. They ate on the balcony, and the conversation, and the wine, flowed freely, and no mention was made of Sybille's property.

At around midnight, Schaerer stretched and yawned. "I'm ready to hit the sack," he said.

"Me too," Sybille said. She drained her glass and got to her feet.

At the door, she gave John a hug. "Let's do that again. I really enjoyed it."

"So did I," John said.

"Wonderful meal, Liz," Sybille said. The fish was cooked to perfection."

"I'm glad you liked it," Liz said.

John saw them out. "Well that went well," he said, after closing the door

"Did it?" Liz said.

"Well I thought it did." He passed Liz some plates so she could load the dishwasher. Then he realised what Liz had said. "Did you not think it went well? She was nice enough, wasn't she?"

"To you, she was; that's for sure."

"What are you talking about?"

"She was all over you."

"When?"

"In the boat, and when we stood on the balcony and looked at the moon."

"Was she?"

"And if I ever see her hug you like that again, I'll scratch her eyes out."

Chapter 10

One morning a week or so later, Liz put the phone down and walked out on to the balcony. "That was Sybille."

John was immersed in an article in the Wall Street Journal. He lowered the paper.

"She's invited me to coffee."

"And are you going?"

"I don't see why not."

"You know what she'll want to talk to you about."

"John, I'm not entirely stupid. I'm going because I'm sick and tired of seeing you moping round with nothing to do."

"Do you want me to come with you?"

"No, thank you."

"Fine." John raised the paper so Liz would not see the smile on his face.

Liz had been gone about two hours and John was lying on the sofa still in his pyjamas. He was reading the latest John Grisham novel. The slatted windows, and sliding door were open, and there was a cooling sea breeze blowing through the apartment. Sybille had picked Liz up, saying she was picking .her up in case John needed the car.

The phone rang. It was Liz. "Sybille is saying she has buyers for some of the apartments."

"And do you believe her?"

"No. But why don't you come over?"

John needed no second bidding. "I'm not dressed yet. Give me an hour."

The Princess Towers hotel was one of Freeport's premier hotels. It was a high-rise building with a Middle Eastern theme. It was a stone's throw from the Straw Market. When John got there, a planeload of Japanese tourists had just arrived and the lobby was full of luggage, and golf bags.

He made his way to the coffee shop. The hotel served breakfast in the coffee shop, and it was busy. He spotted Liz and Sybille at a table by a window overlooking the swimming pool, and made his way over.

Sybille had taken the trouble to wear a suit; an old shiny suit, but a suit nevertheless. She got to her feet. "Good morning, John. "Thank you for coming." She did not offer to shake his hand. She asked a passing waiter to bring coffee, and they made small talk until it arrived.

John took a sip of his coffee, and then said, "So what's this about you having buyers for some of the apartments?"

"I don't have any buyers, John," Sybille said. "I only said that to get you here."

"That's the last time I believe a word *you* say," Liz said.

"I didn't think you had," John said. "No one in their right mind would want to buy an apartment in a property in the condition you've described. But I'll tell you what, Sybille, since we've come this far, why don't you show us the property, and then you won't have to tell us any more lies."

With a small mountain of discarded cookers, fridge-freezers and washing machines in one corner, and a pile of urine-stained mattresses in another, the car park at the property looked better suited to fly tipping than the parking of cars. A dilapidated Cadillac without its wheels was perched on brick plinths, and two other cars; a Pontiac and a Buick, in a similar state of dilapidation, were also perched on bricks. Knee-high weeds sprouted from cracks in the concrete.

John parked beside an ambulance that had its engine running and its rear doors open, and his nose wrinkled at the stench of urine from the pile of mattresses as he stepped out of his car.

Sybille had already parked. They had followed her from the Princess Towers. "Welcome to the property," she said.

"She has to be kidding," Liz muttered.

"Let's give her a chance," John said. "I'm sure it isn't all as bad as this."

Sybille heard him. "It isn't," she said. "Come on, let me show you around."

The moment John stepped on to the property proper, he liked it. It *felt* right.

The property comprised three two-storey buildings set in a U-shaped arrangement around a swimming pool. The middle building ran parallel with the long side of the pool and was about twice the length of the others. The buildings looked tired and sad. The walls, which, at some point in the dim and distant past had been painted white, had rainwater stains running down them, leading John to take a step back to take a look at the roofs. The buildings had pitched roofs made, Sybille said, of Canadian maple shingles, which John would be expensive to replace. Several shingles were missing, and others had curled and would need to be replaced. John made a mental note to look for water stains on the ceilings of the apartments on the upper floor. A close inspection of window frames and door frames, showed many of these to be rotten and in need of replacement.

Sybille then lead them through the gardens, pointing out an avocado tree, a mango tree, and two banana trees. She also pointed out three mature Queen Palm trees, which she said were her favourites. She then led them to what she called her *piece de resistance*, which was the view.

It was truly a view to die for. Behind a row of pine trees, and ringed by beaches of pure white sand with not a soul in sight, was the Atlantic Ocean in all its majesty.

The view alone almost made it worth investing in the property.

"Well, what do you think?" Sybille said.

"It's fabulous," John said, gazing in awe at the view. "Absolutely fabulous."

Even Liz was impressed. Although she wouldn't admit it

Before they took a look at the apartments, they took a look at the swimming pool.

The pool water looked clean and clear, but despite there being people around – some in wheel chairs and many in pyjamas and dressing gown, no one was using it.

John queried Sybille as to why this was.

"Because there's no money for a lifeguard and it's against the law to allow people to swim when there's no lifeguard," Sybille replied.

"Do *you* use it, Sybille?" Liz said.

"All the time. I swim every day, morning and night."

"So the pool is kept in pristine condition just for your benefit," Liz said.

"And why not?" Sybille said, with a self-important shrug. "I'm the manager."

An ambulance man was wheeling an elderly black gentleman in a wheelchair out of his apartment. He was in pyjamas and dressing gown.

"See you when you're feeling better," Sybille said.

The elderly gentleman looked away.

Sybille was using a ground floor apartment as an office. She had left the door and the windows open, but the air was still stifling. John asked her if any of the apartments were air-conditioned.

"Only mine," she said.

"How do terminally-ill people manage without air-conditioning in this heat?" Liz asked.

"I don't know," Sybille said. "You'd have to ask them."

The apartment comprised a decent-sized L-shaped living room/dining room, a small but adequately equipped kitchen, a bedroom which would take a king-sized bed and very little else, and a bathroom which looked as if it had come from the Ark. The apartment was furnished, but the furniture was fit only for dumping.

That was something else John would have to think about if he decided to go ahead with this project. He had learned that residential property in the Bahamas is always sold furnished, and if the furniture in this apartment was anything to go by, it would mean funding new furniture, and carpet, for every apartment.

Sybille had converted the bedroom to an office, but only to the extent that she had installed a metal desk, telephone, and a metal filing cabinet. There was no sign of it ever having been used as an office: no paper, no personal effects, and no knick-knacks. It had as much atmosphere as an empty garage.

John asked her if all the apartments were the same as this one.

"In terms of shape and size, yes, they are."

John had Sybille show him a random selection, selections he made, of some of the apartments on the upper floor, and, as he had feared, a number of them showed signs of water damage. This would mean that, at best, the roofs would have to be repaired. At worst, they would have to be replaced.

Sybille had picked, for herself, the apartment with the very best location. It was on the upper floor at the far end of the long building. From the front, her apartment faced the swimming pool, as did all the apartments, but from the rear she had views, admittedly partly obscured at times by trees, over the ocean. Her apartment looked to have been recently decorated, and her furniture was modern and comfortable-looking. Each room had its own freestanding air-conditioning unit, and they were all running. To John, her apartment was uncomfortably cold, and his thoughts went out to those unfortunate people down below, who, while they waited to die, had to live in ovens.

When he had seen enough they went back to the office.

"Well, what do you think, John?" Sybille said.

"I think the property is exactly as you described it," John replied.

"Does that mean you're interested?"

"What it means, Sybille, is that I need to go away and think about it."

John pulled on to the Grand Bahama Highway, accelerated, and shifted the Grand Cherokee into fifth gear. He had been alone with his thoughts for the last twenty minutes. He finally broke the silence. "Well, what do you think, Liz?"

Liz looked across the vehicle at him. "About Sybille, or the property?"

"Let's start with Sybille."

"I think she's a heartless bitch who lies through her teeth and only thinks of herself. It's disgusting the way she swims every day and won't let any of the patients swim. And as to her excuse that it's against the law to swim without a lifeguard in attendance, that's ridiculous. If that were the case, she shouldn't be swimming either."

"And the property?"

"I wouldn't want to take on all that work, but I suspect you feel otherwise."

"You know something, Liz, it felt right the moment I stepped on to the property. And that view! Wow!"

"Does that mean you're going ahead with it?"

"To the extent that I'm going to have Sybille come up with costings."

"Shouldn't you have costings done yourself?"

"I'll probably end up doing that, but I want to see what she comes up with, first."

"Well, it's your decision, John. All I would say is, rather you than me."

Chapter 11

The maître d' bowed as the group reached the top of the stairs. "Good evening, Mr Humphries. Mrs Humphries."

Humphries nodded. "Uwe."

"Good evening, Uwe," Jill said.

Humphries stepped back to present his guests. "Uwe, this is Mr and Mrs McLaren. They're new to the island and they're good friends of ours, so look after them. Okay?"

"Of course." Uwe bowed to John and Liz. "Welcome to Pier One."

Behind him was a large tank of live lobsters. Their claws were tied; to protect the hands of people who had to pick them up. "I recommend our lobsters. We fly them in fresh from Maine every morning."

"Lobster sounds good to me," John said. "What about you, darling?"

"Yes, but just a small one." Liz peered into the tank. "I'll have that little one, there." She pointed to the smallest lobster in the tank. The crustacean of her choice shifted its position, as if realising its days were numbered.

Uwe nodded to a waiter in a short-sleeved shirt standing by the tank. He had a towel over his arm. He fished out the lobster Liz had chosen, wrapped it in the towel and stood waiting for the others to make their selections.

"Which one do you fancy, John?" Humphries said.

John looked through the glass, then over the rim. He pointed to a lobster weighing probably a couple of pounds. "I'll have that one."

"You gonna have lobster, hon?" Humphries said.

Jill shook her head. "Not tonight. I'm having mahi mahi tonight."

"What's mahi mahi?" Liz said. She said it in a whisper, so as not to appear ignorant to the waiter.

"It's dolphin," Jill said.

"You mean like …"

"Yes, like Flipper."

"I didn't know people ate dolphin."

"Lots of people in these parts eat dolphin. Try some of mine. I think you'll like it."

Humphries pointed to the largest crustacean in the tank. "I'll have that one, the big fella. I'm hungry tonight."

Uwe picked up four leather-backed menus and led the way through the restaurant to the balcony.

As they got to their table, John noticed Rolly Schaerer and Sybille sitting at a table further along the balcony. He excused himself and went to have a word with them.

"Hey there," Schaerer said. "Come to check out the show?"

"Yes, we thought it was time we did. Everyone's been talking about it."

"I didn't know you knew George Humphries."

"He shipped our stuff over from Florida. Liz and I have been seeing quite a bit of them. Good evening, Sybille."

"Hello, John."

"How are the costings coming along?"

"Getting there. I'm just waiting for a third quote on the air-conditioning, then I'm all done."

"Give me a call when you've got everything together. Well, I'd better get back to my party. Nice to see you both."

When John got back to their table, Humphries asked him who the woman was. He said she looked familiar.

"That's Sybille Johanssen," Liz said.

"Ah, okay. I've seen pictures of her on dive boats and stuff. Never had the pleasure to meet her."

"Is she the one with the property?" Jill asked.

"Yes, she's the one," John said.

"So she's the one who believes in witchcraft."

"One and the same," Liz said.

The lobster Humphries had chosen was huge. Its claws were as big as his hands, and he had big hands. He had had it broiled and it was served with mayonnaise and a side salad. John, whose selection was less than half the size, had also had his broiled. Liz had chosen thermidor.

Soon after they started eating, Uwe walked over to ask if everything was to their satisfaction. He topped up their wine glasses.

"It's okay, I guess," Humphries said, shrugging.

"Ignore him, Uwe," Jill said, slapping her husband good-naturedly on the arm. "It's wonderful, as always. George, at least smile when you're winding Uwe up, then he knows you're kidding."

"He knows I'm kidding." Humphries winked at the restaurateur.

"Is the meal to your satisfaction. Mr and Mrs McLaren?"

"It's perfect, Uwe," Liz said. "Thank you. My lobster is delicious."

"Mine too," John said. "It's every bit as good as people said it would be."

"C'mon, guys," Humphries complained. "Don't spoil him. We've gotta keep him on his toes."

Jill gave her husband an exasperated look. "Ignore him, Uwe. What time's show time tonight?"

Uwe looked up at the sky. The light was fading rapidly. "Thirty to forty minutes I would say." He moved to the next table and asked if everything was to their satisfaction.

"Nice that he remembered our names," John said.

"That's one of the reasons he's successful," Humphries said. "He pays attention to detail." He cracked one of his lobster's claws, sending a stream of juice squirting across the table. "Oops, sorry. You had any more thoughts about buying a boat, John?"

John dabbed his lips with his napkin. "I have, actually. I'd like to get one, but as I told you the last time we talked about it, I wouldn't have a clue what to look for. A boat is a boat is a boat, as far as I'm concerned."

"Well, my advice would be to have a word with a guy by the name of Alex Drew. He deals in new, and used, boats. Speaking of which, I would certainly recommend you go for a used boat the first time around. Some people buy a boat on a whim, then find they either never use it, or find that they don't like boating after all, and want to sell it."

"Sounds good to me. How do I make contact with this Alex Drew?"

"I'll look up his number and let you have it."

"What about your sea sickness, John?" Liz said.

"I'll find a way of getting over that."

"Attaboy," Humphries said.

The clanging of a ship's bell less than three feet from his left shoulder left John's ears ringing.

"It's show time," Humphries said. "Better get on your feet if you want to get the best view. They'll be six deep out here in less than twenty seconds."

And he was right. The balcony was heaving almost immediately, as people in the restaurant hurried out to watch the show.

John had been studying the book and when the sharks appeared he was able to identify five different species.

"That was amazing," he said, when the show was over. "I've never seen anything like it. Surprising though that the authorities don't insist on a safety net. It wouldn't take much for someone to fall over the rail."

"Yeah, Uwe wouldn't get away with it in the States, that's for sure," Humphries said. "Dessert, anyone?"

Both John and Liz said they could manage a dessert, just.

"Then I recommend Uwe's Mississippi Mud Pie," Humphries said. "Until you've tried Uwe's Mississippi Mud Pie, you haven't lived."

When they had finished eating their desserts, they were the only people on the balcony, except that is for a waiter who was clearing tables, and Rolly Schaerer and Sybille.

Humphries invited Schaerer and Sybille to join them for coffee.

"Don't mind if we do," Schaerer said.

Humphries summoned the waiter. "Coffees all round, Hank. If you please." He then got up and dragged a couple of chairs over from the next table.

Sybille sat next to Liz. She asked Liz if she had enjoyed the show.

"Very much," Liz said. "You?"

"It was okay. It gets to be old hat when you've seen it as many times as I have."

To John, this sounded like another of Sybille's lies. If she had as little money as she claimed to have, she would hardly be able to afford Uwe's prices.

Jill reached a hand across the table. "We haven't been introduced, Sybille, but I'm Jill. George's wife."

"Sybille Johanssen. Nice to meet you."

"I've been hearing a lot about you recently. You're the one who believes in witchcraft, right?"

"That's right," Sybille said, glancing at Liz. "I'm the one who believes in witchcraft."

John said, "Sybille, I don't believe you've met George Humphries."

"No, I've never had the pleasure, although I know who you are from your BASRA connection. Nice to meet you, George."

"And I know who you are from your UNEXSO connection," Humphries said. "Nice to meet you, too. How are those apartments of yours selling, Rolly?"

"Real well right now, George. An investor flew in from Geneva last week and bought twenty of them. We're on the bubbly tonight to celebrate."

"And why not," John said. "No point making it if you don't enjoy it."

"Amen to that," Humphries said.

Sybille got to her feet. "You ready, Rolly?"

"What's the hurry? We haven't had coffee yet."

"I'll make you one when we get home. Goodnight all." She walked away.

"*Jesus Christ*," Schaerer muttered. "Sorry, guys." He got to his feet.

"Hey, no problem," Humphries said. "You take care, buddy. Okay?"

"Will do," Schaerer said, shaking his head in irritation. He set off after Sybille.

"She makes my skin crawl," Jill said.

"I know what you mean," her husband said. "You sure you're doing the right thing going into business with her, John?"

Chapter 12

George Humphries was as good as his word; he phoned John the next morning and gave him the phone number of the boat dealer. John had a word with the dealer over the phone and then went to see him.

He saw a boat he liked. It was a twenty-two foot sport fishing boat with a centre console and tee-top. It was cream, with brown trim. It was on a trailer.

"Climb aboard and take a look," the dealer said.

John had a problem with claustrophobia in small spaces, even on boats, but the boat had a nice spacious feel to it.

There were padded seats along the sides of the boat, both front and rear – or bow and stern, to use the dealer's terminology – with storage in lockers beneath. And there were deep fish storage lockers at the stern.

John asked the dealer how much he was looking for.

"Give me fifteen grand and she's yours."

"What would a boat like this cost, new?"

"Thirty grand give or take."

"Do you have a brochure?"

"Sure, I have one in my office."

John took brochures on that, and two other boats, home with him. Next morning he went back and told the dealer he would like to order a new version of the boat he had seen the precious day. The boat was listed at $30,125.00.

"You'll never regret buying a boat like that," the dealer said, getting out his order book.

"You'll service and repair it if anything goes wrong."

"Of course. And it'll be under factory guarantee for two years. That price is for the basic boat, trailer and the engine on the boat you saw yesterday. And it includes the import duty. But you're going to need some extras."

"Such as?"

"How much have you budgeted for?"

"$35,000. But that's it, because I'm about to get into a business venture and I don't want to over-commit myself. What do you think I'll need?"

"Well, if you're planning to go offshore, you'll need ship-to-shore radio, and sat nav."

"I'm not planning to circle the globe."

"But you wouldn't want to find yourself lost at sea, would you? There are no landmarks out there."

"You have a point. You'd better make a list."

The dealer licked his pencil. He made a list and handed it to John. "That should do it."

John looked at the list. "You're sure this is within my budget?"

The dealer nodded. "You're within budget."

"What delivery time are we talking about?"

The dealer picked up the phone and spoke to the Florida factory. He put his hand over the mouthpiece. "Fifteen to sixteen weeks."

"Why so long?"

"They've had a fire and production's restricted."

John thought about it for a nanosecond, and then said, "Okay, I think we can live with that. We're not in any particular hurry."

The dealer placed the order and hung up. "You'll need to let me have a $10,000 deposit."

"I'll put a cheque in the mail tonight."

Four days later, the dealer phoned him to inform him that the factory wanted payment in full.

"You're kidding?" John retorted. "Who ever heard of paying for something before they got it?"

"The reason want payment up front is because they don't know you from Adam, and they're saying you might change your mind. It happens when people are buying boats, especially when it's a first boat. They could be stuck with a boat built to your specification."

John was beginning to lose his cool. "Built to *your* specification, you mean."

"You signed the order."

"Yes, but I'm hardly likely to change my mind after I've put a $10,000 deposit on it."

"Well, you won't get the boat if you don't pay up."

"Okay, cancel the order and give me my deposit back."

"I can't do that."

"Why can't you?"

"Because the factory has it. They don't return deposits."

"Come off it. It's an American company. Of course they would return my deposit. What are you up to?"

"I'm not up to anything. You could try suing them."

The last thing John needed at that particular moment in time was to start getting involved in legal fees over a boat. "How much do they want?"

"$32,465."

"But that would mean the boat would be costing $42,465."

"Correct."

"But you said I was within budget, and my budget was $35,000. I was very clear about that."

"That was before you added the extras."

"Bullshit!"

"Well let's put it this way," the dealer said. "You'll lose your deposit, and the boat, unless you cough up the full amount. Let me know what you decide to do." He hung up.

When George Humphries heard what was going on, he was horrified. "Jeez, John, I'm real sorry. And I put you on to the guy."

"It's not your fault," John said. "If I'd taken your advice and gone for a used boat, this would never have happened. George, if I cancelled the order, do you think I would have recourse under Bahamian law?"

"I doubt it," Humphries said. "Since there were no witnesses, it would seem to be your word against his."

John paid up.

Chapter 13

When John responded to a knock at the kitchen door Sybille thrust a slim manila folder at him. "Your costings, John. Sorry, got to go. Things to do." She was down the stairs and into her Nissan 4x4 before he even had time to thank her.

As he leafed through the quotes, John saw that Sybille had done what she had said she was doing: getting quotes on each job from three different contractors. And she had presented them in a businesslike fashion. What she had not done was provide a summary as to what the overall job would cost.

It was when he found himself a pad and pencil and added everything up that he realised why she had not wanted to hang around. Her quotes added up to a cool half million dollars.

Investing over half a million dollars in the property was out of the question. It wasn't that the money wasn't available; it was just that it was too big a chunk of what he had in his account in Nassau to risk. He had been carrying Jack Smith's business card in his wallet since the Canadian had given it to him at the barbecue, and he took it out and called him.

Smith laughed when John told him what Sybille had come up with. "That's an old trick," he said. "She's taking backhanders and, by the sound of it, pretty big ones. I'll give Randy Exton a call. He's from Texas. Drive him to the property and tell him what you need."

Exton called John later that day and they set up a date and time.

John told Sybille he would be bringing someone to look at the property, but he didn't say why. But Sybille sussed what was going on and never had so many apartment keys been turned in such anger. John and the Texan exchanged grins on several occasions.

Sybille had hardly said a word. She hadn't needed to. Her face had said it all.

"Well, what do you think, Randy?" John said, as they walked back to the Jeep.

Exton turned and took a brief last look at the property. "I reckon I can do it for two-fifty grand. Two-seventy, tops."

"The whole thing? New roofs; air-conditioning in every apartment; replacing rotten woodwork; painting and decorating; new carpets; furniture, clearing the site and carting everything away?"

"The whole thing."

"How long do you think it would take?"

"It shouldn't take longer than …sixteen to eighteen weeks. It's not a big job."

"And how soon could you start?"

"I have a couple of other jobs to finish first, but I could start in, say, a month from today."

"Would you let me have a quote in writing? It's not that I don't trust you or anything, but…"

"Hey, no sweat. I would want it in writing too if I was spending that kind of money."

The Texan's quote arrived in the mail three days later. The overall cost was less than half what Sybille had quoted. Payment was to be made by an up-front payment of twenty-five percent, a further twenty-five percent six weeks after the job had started, and the balance to be paid on completion to the client's satisfaction.

John phoned the Texan and thanked him for his quote. He told him he needed to sleep on it, but would get back to him within a couple of days.

"No sweat," the Texan said. "You have my number."

That night John slipped quietly out of bed, put on a T-shirt and a pair of shorts and walked down to the beach.

A full moon cast shards of light over water as still as a millpond.

73

It wasn't the thought of investing so much money in the project that was keeping him awake, because he knew it could turn into an excellent investment. It was more what Liz was thinking that was worrying him. She had been keeping her cards close to her chest recently and the last thing he wanted was something to go wrong with his marriage after all he and Liz had been through. They had been married over thirty years.

Liz was up when he got back to the apartment. She hadn't been sleeping either. She handed him a towel to wipe the sand off his feet.

"Coffee?" she said.

"That would be nice."

With her feet tucked up beneath her, and a mug of coffee in her hand, Liz said, "Okay, John, out with it. What's bothering you?"

John put his mug on a magazine on the coffee table, and came right out with it. "What's bothering me, Liz, is going ahead with Sybille knowing how you feel about her."

Liz nodded. "I thought that was probably what it was."

"I want you to know, Liz, that if I do go ahead with her, I would never give you cause to regret it. You have always been my priority and you always will be."

Liz smiled at him. "I know that, John, and that's why I want you to go ahead with it. I know that's what you want to do."

"You're sure, Liz? You're absolutely sure?"

"Yes, I'm sure. I'm absolutely sure."

John felt the tension ebbing from his neck. "Wow, what a relief. I hadn't known how to talk to you about it."

The next morning, John phoned Randy Johnson and accepted his quote, and then he and Liz drove to the property to break the news to Sybille.

When they got out of the car, there was a sound like a parrot screeching. It was Sybille. She was standing by the pool with her hands on her hips and her legs akimbo and she was berating the elderly gardener. The poor man was standing there

with a rake in his hand, his head down and his shoulders drooping.

"I wonder what he's done to deserve that," Liz said.

"Knowing her, probably nothing," John replied.

"Are you sure you want to go ahead with her, John? You could give back word to Randy Johnson. I'm sure he wouldn't mind at this early stage."

John shook his head. "I don't want to do that. It's only for a year. I can live with it for a year."

Sybille spotted them and called, "Be right with you."

They waited for her in the office.

Sybille walked in and smiled. "I wasn't expecting you two today. How are you both?"

"We're fine," Liz said.

"We have some news for you," John said.

Sybille's ears twitched. "Good news, I hope." She perched on the arm of the sofa.

"Some good, some bad," John said. "Which do you want first?"

"I'm not sure I like the sound of bad news, but why don't we get that out of the way first?'

"Well, the bad news is that we're not going ahead with the quotes you came up with. They were far too high."

If Sybille was upset by this news, she didn't show it. "And the good news?"

"We're going ahead with the deal, but using Randy Johnson."

Sybille shrugged. "It's your money. So where do we go from here?"

"The next step is probably for us to meet the owner," John said.

Sybille frowned. "Why do you need to meet him? I speak for him."

"We only have your word for that," Liz said.

Sybille's eyes flashed. "Are you suggesting that ..."

"Do you have his enduring power of attorney?" John asked.

"No, but ..."

"Then we need to meet him?"

"And what if I can't arrange it? As I told you, he's an old man. He lives in Florida, and he doesn't travel."

"Sybille," Liz snapped, "why the hell do you have to make a drama out of everything?"

"Don't you talk to me like ..."

"You're right, Liz," John said, getting to his feet. "It isn't too late to pull out. Come on, let's go and find something else to invest our money in."

"All right, all right," Sybille said hastily. "Keep your hair on. I'll arrange a meeting."

Chapter 14

For their meeting with the owner of the property, Sybille had booked a table for lunch at the Xanadu Beach Hotel.

The hotel overlooked a beach, and a canal with a dock, and it just so happened that an international tuna fishing competition was being held that day.

They were early and they wandered down to the dock to take a look.

There was good-natured banter and much slapping of backs as men who had known each other for years renewed their acquaintance and had their catches weighed.

George Humphries was there with his boat *Catch Me If You Can* and they spent a few minutes chatting with him. A couple of the fish on his boat were still twitching.

Until then, tuna had been something you bought in a tin from a shop, and this was a real eye-opener for them. Even the small ones were weighing in at over a hundred and fifty pounds.

In the restaurant, the maître d' showed them to a table overlooking the dock. Sybille had set the time of the meeting for 1:00 p.m., but by 1:30 she had still not arrived. They had a glass of house wine while they waited.

"You'd think she'd be on time for a meeting as important as this," Liz said, running her finger up and down the stem of her glass.

"Perhaps his flight was delayed," John said.

Sybille strolled in at 2:15 with a shambling bear of a man. She was carrying a battered old briefcase. "Hi there," she said. "Not late are we?"

"Not unless you call an hour and fifteen minutes, late," John muttered, under his breath.

He wondered why Sybille had chosen such an elegant, and expensive, venue for the meeting. They could just as easily have met on the property. But his was not to reason why. He wasn't paying.

"John, may I present Enrico Rodrigues." She put her mouth to the big man's ear and bawled, "Enrico, this is John McLaren, and his wife, Elizabeth."

"Very nice to meet you, Mr Rodrigues," John said.

Rodrigues mumbled something unintelligible.

When they had all sat down, Sybille explained that she had to shout because Rodrigues was profoundly deaf. She put her mouth to the big man's ear, and yelled, "I was just telling them, Enrico, that you're profoundly deaf and that's why I have to shout."

"Yeah, but we ain't deaf, lady," a man at the next table said. "So how about turning down the volume?"

"And how about you moving to another table?" Sybille retorted.

Throughout the meal, Rodrigues looked vague; as if he didn't know where he was, or why he was there.

"Is he for real?" Liz whispered.

"Search me," John whispered back.

Every time one of them asked a question, Sybille answered it. Then she yelled in the big man's ear and told him what she had said to them.

People were beginning to complain about the noise, and the maître d' looked on the point of coming over to speak to them.

Sybille ploughed on regardless.

"I've told them we don't need to give cash up front, and that you'll let us do what we want with the property in exchange for four thousand dollars a month."

"S'right," the big man mumbled.

The man who had complained about the noise leaned over and tapped John on the shoulder. "I sure hope you know what you're doing, pal."

"That makes two of us," John said.

Liz nudged him. "This is ridiculous. She's answering all the questions for him."

Spittle was dribbling from the big man's mouth. Sybille dabbed at it with his napkin, and then dropped the napkin on the floor as if it were contaminated with a virus. She bent down, opened her briefcase and took out a document. She handed it to John. "You might want to take a look at this."

The document was headed: In The Matter Of Atlantic Beach Apartments, Freeport and Enrico Rodrigues, Sybille Johanssen, and John and Elizabeth McLaren.

John read the document when they got home. It was the first draft of an agreement in which Enrico Rodrigues gave them permission to do as they wished with the property in exchange for a monthly payment of $4,000. The agreement stated that payments were to begin on the day all four parties had signed the agreement, and were to continue until the last apartment had been sold. John looked for the get-out clause, and the get-out clause in this document specified that, in the event of default in payment for a period of three months, they would be held in breach of contract. Then, if within a further three months they failed to rectify this breach, the agreement would be declared null and void, meaning that the property would revert to Enrico Rodrigues.

John found nothing contentious in the agreement; nothing he couldn't live with, after a little tweaking here and there. He phoned Sybille and asked her to set up a meeting with Enrico's lawyer.

Nicholas Truckle turned out to be a fit-looking Haitian in his early to mid-forties. He was a fully-fledged barrister. He was dressed in the manner in which barristers at the Inns of Court in London dressed: black jacket, white shirt with grey silk tie, and grey pinstripe trousers. His office was decorated with an impressive array of framed certificates. He insisted on them calling him Nicholas and his business card revealed him to be a full partner in the firm.

They chatted for a while, to get to know each other, and it soon became apparent that he knew the UK well, having been educated at Harrow. He told them he had graduated in law at Harvard. He and John then spent twenty minutes or so working on the wording of the agreement.

Finally, John said he was happy with it.

"Good, I'll have it formalised in time for our next meeting."

"I have a question," John said. "Does Enrico have clear title to the property? I wouldn't want to get into this if he didn't."

"You have my absolute assurance, John, that he does have clear title to the property." He handed John another document. "This is not essential, but we recommend that everybody starting a legal entity signs one of these. It's the standard form of partnership agreement."

John gave the one-page document the once over. It was simply to say that the partners would at all times treat each other with courtesy, respect and consideration. He had no hesitation in signing it.

Liz signed next.

John wondered if Sybille would have the brass neck to sign it, since she never, ever observed such niceties.

It spoke volumes about Sybille that she signed it without giving it a second thought.

The lawyer put the document in a folder. "Now," he said, "does anyone have anything they would like to say?"

"I have nothing I want to say, as such," Sybille said. "But I need to ask how much I'll be getting paid."

John looked at her, puzzled. "For doing what?"

"I don't know," Sybille said. "I can put my mind to virtually anything. But I can't live on nothing."

"Why should we pay you anything?" Liz said. "You're a partner, I'm a partner, and John's a partner, and John and I are not getting paid."

"Yes, but you have money," Sybille said. "I don't."

"Sybille has a point," the lawyer said. "She can't live on nothing."

"What kind of money are we talking about?" John said.

"Enrico was paying me $1,000 a week."

John turned to the lawyer. "Is this true, Nicholas?"

"I think perhaps I should stay out of this," the lawyer said.

"And I'll want to continue to live on the property," Sybille said.

"I have no problem with that," John said. "We'll need a caretaker anyway."

"Then I'll be the caretaker," Sybille said enthusiastically. "And you don't get caretakers for nothing."

"And you don't pay them a thousand dollars a week either," Liz said.

"How would *you* know?" Sybille snapped. "When did *you* last employ a caretaker?"

"Ladies, *please*," John said.

"If I might make a suggestion," the lawyer said. "Perhaps $500 a week would be workable, especially since Sybille will not have to pay rent."

"I can live with that," John said.

"Can you live with that, Sybille?" the lawyer said.

"It looks like I'm going to have to. But I can't say I'm ..."

"Moving swiftly on," the lawyer said, rubbing his hands together briskly. "Is there any other business?"

"There is one thing," Sybille said. "I don't want Liz being a director of the company."

"Why not?" John said sharply.

"Because I know what she thinks of me and I'm not having the two of you ganging up on me all the time."

John had an idea. "Nicholas, is it possible in the Bahamas that a legal entity has just one director."

"It is, John, but ..."

"That won't work for me," Sybille said. "I want to be a director. In fact, I insist on it."

"You're not in a position to insist on anything," Liz said.

"May I ask why being a director is so important to you," the lawyer said.

"I have my reasons."

"All right," Liz said, "if you and John are going to be directors, I'm going to be a director too."

"Over my dead body," Sybille said.

"Don't tempt me," Liz said.

"Ladies, *please*," John said.

Sybille sighed and got to her feet. "I've had enough of this." She flounced out of the room, slamming the door behind her.

For the next couple of minutes the only sound was the ticking of the grandfather clock in the corner and the muffled sound of traffic from the street below. They half-expected Sybille to come back, but she didn't.

The lawyer finally broke the silence. "Liz, may I ask why you feel the need to be a director?"

"I don't. Call it point scoring, if you like."

"Well, I don't blame you for that, but to put this in perspective, it's who owns the property that matters. With John also speaking for your ownership, he will control two thirds of the company and with him behind you, you could veto anything and everything Sybille wanted to do, and there would be nothing she could do about it."

"Come on, Liz," John said. "Let's not blow it out of the water at this stage. We're almost there."

"I don't know, John. There's always something. I'm still not sure we should be getting involved with her."

"Darling, it's only for a year, then we'll be shot of her. Please, do this for me. You know how long it's taken me to find something."

"All right, John," Liz said finally. "But on your head be it."

Chapter 15

An agenda had been sent to each participant in advance of the next meeting with the lawyer.

There were five people at the meeting, which was held in the conference room of the law firm's suite of offices. These were: Enrico Rodrigues, John, Liz, Sybille, and the lawyer himself.

Nicholas Truckle's English secretary, Christine, was on hand to witness signatures and take down the minutes of the new company's first board meeting.

The first item on the agenda was the resignation of Enrico Rodrigues as director of Atlantic Beach Apartments, Ltd.

John had been wondering how Enrico was managing to make these trips from Florida in his delicate state of health, and Sybille informed him that his niece, Sarah, with whom he lived in Florida, had been accompanying him. They had been staying overnight on the property.

Since Sybille was likely to be tied up for some time, Sarah was in the reception area waiting to take him to the airport for their flight back to Miami.

Truckle called the meeting to order.

"The first item is – he raised his voice to a yell – *Enrico, you resigning your directorship in the company.*"

The paperwork had been completed in advance and all it required was the big man's signature, which he accomplished with the help of the lawyer's Mont Blanc fountain pen, and a very shaky hand.

The lawyer Truckle had not seen his client's signature for some considerable time, and it was virtually unrecognisable.

He had his client sign again, below the original signature, to be on the safe side.

Christine witnessed the two signatures, printing out her full name and home address after her signature.

The lawyer then yelled, "*All we need from you now, Enrico, is one more signature, and then Sarah can take you to the airport.*"

This document needed all three of them to sign.

Christine witnessed them and then left the room to call a taxi to take Enrico and his niece to the airport. They waited until she returned and then got back to the matter at hand.

"Item two on the agenda is the election of John and Sybille as directors of the company." In case Liz had had a change of heart about becoming a director, the lawyer paused to give her the opportunity to speak up. When no comment was forthcoming, he said, "John, I've put you down as chairman."

"Fine with me."

The lawyer handed him a form to sign. "Sybille, you need to sign this, too."

They signed where indicated, and Christine witnessed their signatures.

"Who wants to be company secretary? A thankless job, but somebody has to do it."

"You can put me down for that," Liz said. "That way I can keep control of the purse strings."

Sybille's brow darkened, but she wisely kept her counsel.

The meeting proceeded smoothly.

Finally, the lawyer said, "Right, I think that's it. Unless one of you has something to add."

"Shouldn't we be having a board meeting?" Liz said.

"We've just had it," the lawyer said, smiling at her. "If you type up the minutes, Christine, these good people can be on their way. They have a bank account to set up."

For the company bank account John had chosen the Freeport branch of the Nassau bank in which he had deposited their capital. To him, this made perfect sense, since it should mean that transfers between the two accounts could be made quickly and with a minimum of fuss.

Andy McTavish, the manager of the Freeport branch, was a self-effacing Scot from Aberdeen. Coincidentally, he played golf to the same eight-handicap as John. He got everyone seated and congratulated them on their new venture. He got some forms out of his desk drawer.

"Which of you has been appointed company secretary?"

"I have," Liz said.

"Did you bring the minutes of the board meeting?"

Liz handed them over.

McTavish cast an expert eye over the minutes and then handed Liz a form to complete. "I'm afraid there's quite a lot of it, but take your time. And don't hesitate to ask if you need any help."

Liz got her pen from her handbag and set to work.

"And the directors are?"

"Me and John," Sybille said.

"Yes, Sybille and I," John confirmed.

McTavish handed John a form. "You need to sign on the dotted line, John. Sybille, sign below John's signature."

They signed accordingly.

"I assume you'll want two signatures on the cheques, John."

"I think we should," John said.

"And who will the signatories be?"

"Me and John," Sybille said.

"They will not," Liz said hotly. "You're not signing cheques."

"May I remind you you're speaking to a director of the company," Sybille said indignantly.

Liz threw back her head and laughed. "Grow up, Sybille."

"Liz will be counter-signing the cheques," John said.

"So be it." McTavish entered the names on a form and handed it to Liz. "Sign against your name, Liz. And, John, you need to do the same. And sign as you would normally sign a cheque, because these will be used as your specimen signatures."

Liz signed the form and passed it to John and then got back to completing the form she had been working on. She came to a question she couldn't answer and looked up. "Sybille, does the property have another bank account?"

"You'll need to close it, if it has, Sybille," McTavish said. "By Bahamian law, a company is not allowed to have a bank account with another bank unless mandated by the board of directors, which is clearly not the case here."

"I'll close it tomorrow," Sybille said.

"As a matter interest, Sybille, where is the other account?" John asked this out of pure curiosity.

"As I said, I'll close it tomorrow."

"Make sure you do," John said, miffed. "I'm not having us start our new venture on the wrong side of the law."

Liz completed the form she had been working on, and signed it. She handed it to McTavish.

The banker checked it through, and then handed it to John. "Sign where it says director. You too, Sybille."

They signed accordingly.

"John, I understand you'll be transferring money into the new account."

"Yes, I need you to transfer fifty thousand dollars from our Nassau account. Then we can get started on the renovations."

"Right, I'll prepare the paperwork. Perhaps you would drop in tomorrow to sign it. The money will be transferred today. Meantime, I'll issue you with temporary cheques. Your chequebooks should be with you within the week. Does anyone have any questions?"

"There's the matter of my weekly stipend," Sybille said.

"I'll cut you a cheque once a week," Liz said. "Or we can set up a standing order and have it paid straight into your bank account. Either way works for me."

"I'd rather have cash."

"I'm not having that kind of money lying around on the property," John said. "And I certainly don't propose to invest in a safe."

"Which means that John or I would have to come to the bank to get it for you," Liz said.

"Well you've got a car, haven't you?"

"I'll pretend I didn't hear that," Liz said.

The banker had a suggestion to make. "Why don't we set up an arrangement here at the bank for Sybille to drop in once a week and collect her money?"

"That sounds like an excellent idea," John said. "Would that work for you, Sybille?"

Sybille smirked at Liz. "That would work just fine. Thank you, John. Thank you very much."

Chapter 16

John ended the conversation and put the phone down. "Shit!" he muttered. "Shit, shit, shit, shit, shit, shit, shit."

Liz was rattling around putting the breakfast dishes away. "Are you ready for another cup of coffee, John?"

John was so engrossed in the ramifications of what he had just heard that he didn't hear her. He stepped out on to the balcony and stood at the rail.

There was muted conversation and the rattle of crockery from the hotel. A seagull flew past, startling him.

He was sorry about Randy, very sorry, because he had liked him, and he was ever sorrier for Randy's family, but why yesterday, of all days? The very day they signed the agreement and opened the company bank account. *Jesus Christ*!

Liz stepped out on to the balcony and slipped her arm through his. "Didn't you hear me, darling? I asked you if you were ready for another cup of coffee."

"No, sorry. I didn't. I was miles away."

"You look like someone who just lost the winning ticket to the lottery."

"That's not a bad analogy, actually."

"Is it something to do with the phone call you've just taken?"

"Yes, it is."

"Who was it?"

"Jack Smith."

"What did he want?

John sighed. "To tell me Randy Exton was killed in a boating accident yesterday."

"But that's awful. Did he have a family?"

"I don't know, Liz. We didn't talk family. But that's beside the point. The point is that we now have no one to do the renovations for us. You know something, Liz? It's one damn thing after another. It's almost as if there's someone up there looking down on me and telling me I've just made a huge mistake getting involved in this project."

"What are you going to do?"

"Right now, I haven't got a clue. But I do know one thing; if I don't have a strategy when I break the news to Sybille, she'll eat me alive."

"Sit down, John," Liz said. "There's something I need to say."

They sat at the table on the balcony.

"John, I know we need to think about ourselves first, because it's our money we're talking about, but I wouldn't want to be responsible for Enrico having no income when the hospital removes the cancer patients from the property. It's not his fault this tragedy's happened, and, from what I understand, we would still make a profit if we went ahead using Sybille's quotes."

"There's something you're overlooking, darling. If we go ahead with Sybille's quotes, we'll have to put down $215,000 in advance, and if anything goes wrong, and anything's possible when you're working with someone like Sybille, we could lose it."

"Do you think Jack Smith was right? About her taking kick backs, I mean."

"I think it's entirely possible. I need to put my thinking cap on. Why don't you make that coffee?"

John gave himself twenty-four hours to work out a strategy.

When they got to the property, Sybille was standing outside the office watching the gardener mow the lawn. She had a huge smile on her face. It was rare to see her even crack a smile these days.

"I wonder what she's looking so pleased about," Liz said. She looks like the cat that got the cream."

"She won't be smiling when she hears what I have to say," John said. "Good morning, Sybille."

"Good morning, partners." Sybille beamed at them, as if they were her favourite people in the whole wide world.

"Let's go inside," John said. "We need to talk."

Sybille's smile faltered. "I'm not sure I like the sound of that."

They followed her into the apartment. "Coffee?" she said. They both replied in the affirmative.

Liz plonked herself down in one of the lumpy armchairs.

John stood by the kitchen door so he could talk to them simultaneously while Sybille made the coffee. "Have you heard the news?" he said.

"If you mean about Randy Exton, yes I've heard. I heard soon after it happened."

"So you've had time to think about it," John said.

"You're point being?"

"You've probably worked out that, since Randy is no longer in the picture, we'll have to use your quotes."

"The thought had crossed my mind."

"Well, I hate to burst your bubble, Sybille," John said, " but it ain't going to happen."

Sybille looked at him in surprise, all thought of making coffee now forgotten. "But the only other people who can quote are the people who have already quoted me. Besides, you're committed. You signed the agreement."

"Which, if that's what you think, you need to read again. And read it properly this time."

"What on earth are you getting at?" Sybille's frown resembled a ploughed field.

"I mean, Sybille, that the agreement clearly states that if we don't make the monthly payments to Enrico, we will be in breach of the agreement in three months' time, following which we have a further three months to rectify the breach. Failing that, the property reverts to him. According to my reckoning, six months at $1,000 a month works out to $24,000, which is all we would be committed to if we didn't go ahead.

If, on the other hand, we go ahead with your quotes, not only will it be nip and tuck as to whether we make a profit at all ...'

"Which is bullshit, and you know it."

"But we also have to pay $215,000 in advance, some of which you would no doubt get your hot sticky fingers on ..."

"I'm sure I don't know what you're talking about. And I resent the implication ..."

"And it would be lost to us forever."

"But Enrico would have no income. You can't do that to him. That wouldn't be fair."

"Come off it, Sybille," Liz called, from the other room. "Don't try to pretend you're interested in Enrico's welfare. From the very beginning, all you've been interested in is yourself."

"A girl has to look after herself," Sybille muttered, almost to herself. "I mean, what the hell? But seriously, John, you wouldn't pull out at this stage would you? I mean ..."

"I don't want to pull out, Sybille, and there is another way."

"Which is?"

"That you come up with a set of quotes that match the quote Randy Exton came up with."

"But I'm not privy to what he quoted."

"And there's no reason why you should be. Let's say you have a ceiling of ... $250,000."

"I don't know about that, John. That's a long way from ..."

"No problem," John said. "Liz, why don't you and I go and find ourselves something else to spend our money on?"

"I do wish you'd stop saying that," Sybille said. "All right. I'll see what I can do."

Chapter 17

"John, I've just heard some disturbing news." The concern was evident in the lawyer's voice. "Sybille tells me you're planning to pull out of the deal."

"In which case, Nicholas, she's being, shall we say, economical with the truth. Because that's the last thing on my mind."

"I'm glad to hear it, John, because it would put Enrico in a very difficult position financially if you did pull out."

"I know, and we won't be pulling out. You'll understand when I say I rely on your discretion not to pass that on to Sybille."

"Of course."

"She knows what she has to do, Nicholas, and I'm sorry that she saw fit to waste your time."

While they waited for Sybille's quotes, John and Liz behaved like a couple on holiday. They played golf, they swam, they fished, they snorkelled. They ate out several times a week, twice with George and Jill Humphries, and once with Rolly Schaerer who, he said, was taking a well-earned break from Sybille. And they drove from one end of the island to the other, exploring inlets and beaches, most of which were deserted.

Sybille brought the new quotes round one morning when they were just about to take their morning dip in the ocean. When Liz answered the door in her bathing costume, Sybille apologised and asked if she had come at a bad time.

Liz shook her head. "It's okay. Did you want to see John?"

Sybille looked close to tears. "Liz, I know I've behaved badly in the past, but if I promise to behave myself in the future, can we start again? *Please.*" There was a look of desperation on her face.

"Who is it?" John called.

"It's Sybille."

John came to the door. "Good morning," he said.

"Good morning, John. I hope I haven't come at an inconvenient time."

John gestured at the buff-coloured file folder she was carrying. "Is that what I think it is?"

Sybille nodded. "The new quotes, yes."

"Am I going to like them?"

"I think so." She laughed self-consciously. "I hope so."

"What's the bottom line?"

When Sybille told him how much it was going to cost him, John nodded. "How much up front?"

"There's nothing up front. You pay for each job when it's been completed."

"You see what you can do when you try, Sybille?" John put his hand out. "Leave them with me."

With the cancer patients gone, ergo no movement to distract the eye, the property looked more dilapidated than ever. But the lawn had been cut and the pool water looked so inviting that John was tempted to strip off to his boxer shorts and take a dip. Knowing that he had, finally, achieved his objective, he felt a sense of euphoria. Now he couldn't wait to make a start on improving the place.

Sybille was in the office with the door open. She heard them talking and came out. "Did I get it right this time?" she asked hopefully.

John nodded. "You got it right this time, so well done. Now, we've wasted enough time, so let's get on with it."

Chapter 18

As the renovations began, John realised that, had Randy Exton handled them, he would have been left with nothing to do but observe. As it was, he had what he had been looking for all along, which was a hands-on project.

Someone had to be on hand to answer the contractors' questions and pull everything together, and that someone had to be him. It certainly couldn't be Sybille; she was hopeless with people. All she did was interfere and annoy everyone.

John had a clear vision of how he wanted the property to look, and he had made it clear to Sybille from the outset that this was his project and that he would be making the decisions.

"Be my guest," Sybille had said with a shrug. "If you want to pay me five hundred bucks a week for doing nothing, that's fine by me."

John was on the property all day and every day, and, because he had had the car park cleared first, he saw an improvement from day one. The old cars had been hauled away and the piles of stinking mattresses and discarded kitchen appliances had been carted off to the dump. What was left was a third of an acre of concrete with weeds sprouting from the cracks, and oil stains. He had plans to resurface the car park and have the whole area professionally landscaped, but for the moment he had the gardener treat the weeds with a powerful weed killer. Now, at least, the contractors had somewhere to park their vehicles.

The roofing contractor, a genial Bahamian, had brought two crews. One crew ripped off the old shingles, while the other crew, working a few paces behind them, hammered on the new ones. They were using Canadian red cedar shingles.

John had heard it said that Bahamian males never actually grow up, that they remain boys forever, and this was borne out by the crew removing the old shingles and flinging them like Frisbees to see who could fling them furthest. John had found this quite amusing at first but, when the gardener had to start fishing shingles out of the pool, he had to tell the contractor to tell his men to cease and desist.

John had thought to put the pool cover on while work was going on, but when he mentioned this to Sybille; she looked at him as if he were stupid. "If you think I'm fooling with the fucking cover every time I want a swim, you can think again."

Debris lay everywhere and walking on the grass in bare feet was a definite no-no. John had asked the clearance contractor, an irascible man of Haitian descent, to come in twice a week, but the man had refused point-blank. His contract stipulated once a week, and once a week it was going to be, come hell or high water. He came in late on a Friday afternoon, which meant that the gardens were only ever free of debris during the weekend. From Monday to Friday, they resembled a war zone.

Sybille was happy enough with this arrangement. It meant she could swim at the weekend without fear of stepping on something sharp.

John took to arriving on the property around 10:00 a.m. and leaving around noon for a sandwich at home with Liz. In the afternoon, he would return around 2:00 p.m. and leave around 4:00 p.m., when the contractors usually left.

Liz hardly ever joined him on the property. It was his project and she was happy to let him get on with it. Occasionally, when she needed a vehicle, she would drop him off and pick him up later. She rarely saw Sybille. Deliberately, John suspected.

From the outset, Sybille vented her spleen on anyone who crossed her, except John. She treated him with the utmost respect. She yelled at the employees with impunity, because no one had the guts to stand up to her.

One day, she picked on the wrong man. He was a huge Bahamian and he was installing new windows. He had had the gall to leave a piece of equipment where Sybille didn't think he should have left it, and she was yelling at him to shift it, or else. "Or else what, lady?" the big man growled. He took a step towards her. Sybille fled. Progress on the site was halted momentarily as workmen had a good laugh at Sybille's expense.

Next on John's list was to have the walls of the buildings pressure-washed.

He was standing outside the office with Sybille one day when she absentmindedly pulled up her sleeve and scratched her arm. He was shocked to see track marks and ugly purple bruises. When he came to think about it later, he realised he had rarely seen Sybille in anything other than long-sleeved clothes. Now he knew why. She was clearly an addict, and this could go a long way towards explaining her behaviour and her mood swings.

She realised he had seen. "So now you know," she said, pulling her sleeve down.

What Sybille chose to inject into her veins was none of his business, but John genuinely wanted to help, if she would let him. He asked her if she wanted to talk about it.

"I don't mind talking about it," she said, with a slight shrug of her shoulders. "But it won't help."

There were two deckchairs in the shade of the mango tree and they walked over and sat in them.

"How long have you been taking drugs, Sybille?'

"I don't remember exactly, but a long time. I was taking them in Canada."

"Do you mind my asking what you're on?"

There was a noise like an amplified dentist's drill from one of the buildings. One of the air-conditioning fitters was using a tool with an industrial diamond tip to cut a hole in a window.

"Heroin, crack cocaine. Whatever I can get."

A jet bearing the livery of Air Canada flew high overhead. It was making vapour trails in the clear blue sky. It was heading northeast, probably heading home to Toronto. There were regular flights between Toronto and Nassau. Nassau was just a short flight from Freeport.

"How can you afford drugs on $500 a week?"

"I can't. Without putting too fine a point on it, I've had to resort to prostitution. I've become a hooker, just like my mother." A flash of anger crossed her face.

"*Jesus Christ*, Sybille! Why didn't you say something?"

"Would it have made a difference?"

She had a point; it wouldn't have made a difference. There was no way he would give her money to feed her habit.

She sat up in her deckchair and turned to him. Her eyes were pleading with him. "Please, John. Even if it's only just a little bit more."

He shook his head. "I'm sorry, Sybille."

"I would make it worth your while." She put her hand on his arm.

"I don't think so, Sybille."

She removed her hand. "Then would you loan me some money. I'd pay you back after we'd sold the first apartment. I promise. *Please*, John."

This was getting tiresome. "Sybille, if you need money, you should go to your bank."

"I've already been to my bank."

"Then give Andy McTavish a try. He knows you have a fifty percent stake in the property, and he knows you'll have money when we start selling the apartments. He'll probably be only too happy to help."

"I've already tried him. He turned me down."

That was a surprise. While Sybille probably didn't have much of a credit rating, he would have thought McTavish would be only too pleased to help. "Did he say why?"

"No, he didn't. And he seemed in a pretty big hurry to get rid of me."

"That's odd. I wonder why that would be. I'll have a word with him."

When John told McTavish why he had wanted to see him, the banker looked visibly relieved. "I'm glad you've brought this up, John," he said. "Because I've been losing sleep over how I was going to tell you. The fact of the matter is, three members of staff have reported seeing Sybille on drug boats and, if Nassau thought this branch was loaning money to people involved in drug running, I would be on the next plane back to Aberdeen."

When Sybille asked him how he had got on at the bank, John shook his head. "Sorry, nothing doing."

"Did he say why?"

"He did, but I'd rather not say."

"Oh, for Christ's sake, John! I'm not a child."

"All right then, he thinks you're involved in running drugs."

"Why would he think that?"

"Because three members of his staff have seen you on drug boats."

"Then somebody doesn't know the difference between dive boats and drug boats. I'm out on dive boats all the time. You know that."

"Well, that's what he said."

"John, let me ask you a question. If I were involved in running drugs, why would I have no money?"

John had no answer to that.

For the rest of that day, Sybille was hell on legs. She gave the air-conditioning fitters such a hard time that they threatened to walk off the job. And he could see that they meant it. He had an idea.

That evening he asked Liz if she was still interested in learning to scuba dive.

"Very much so," she said. "Why do you ask?"

"Because I have a problem, and I think you might be able to help solve it."

"Do tell."

John explained about his problem with the air-conditioning fitters. "And I thought that if you took up Sybille's offer, it would get her off the property."

"How much time are we talking about?"

"Two days. Three at the most."

Liz pulled a face. "I don't know, John. Three days would be a long time to be alone with Sybille. I think I'd rather spend three days in a tank of sharks."

"It *is* for a good cause, Liz."

Liz spent a moment or two mulling it over, and then she said, "Oh, all right. But you'll owe me big time."

John gained gold star brownie points with the fitters for getting Sybille off the property, and he almost got a standing ovation when he told them they could use the pool during their lunch break. Sybille had always refused to allow them to use it.

For the next three days, Liz made John sandwiches and he stayed on the property. By the end of the third day, the fitters had finished the job and had upped and left. It was well after six, by which time Sybille would normally have been back, so John locked the office and left for the day.

When he got home, he walked into a frosty, "I've got a bone to pick with you."

He looked at her blankly. "Sorry?"

"Sybille told me you propositioned her."

"You're kidding!"

"No, I'm not."

"Liz, I wouldn't fancy her if she were the last woman on the planet."

"Well, that's what she told me."

John headed for the fridge to get out a bottle of wine. "That's probably because I refused to give her more money."

He got out two wine glasses and set about taking the cork out of the bottle. "And to set the record straight, *she* propositioned *me*, not the other way round."

Liz tossed the cloth she had been angrily wiping the worktop with into the sink. "I'll be on the balcony."

A booze cruise lurked a hundred yards offshore. It was packed. The music had not yet started.

John handed Liz a glass of wine and sat down. "Liz, tell me you believe me." He sipped his wine.

Liz studied her wine. "How do I know what the two of you get up to on the property? You could be at it like rabbits for all I know."

"What, with Sybille? Do me a favour. Liz, have I ever given you reason to doubt me?"

"You've had your moments."

"And you've had yours. Exactly what did she say?"

"She said she asked you for more money, and that you told her you would give it to her if she slept with you. She told me she was shocked. She said she didn't know you were like that."

"And I'm supposed to work with her, after this?"

Loud reggae music began on the boat. Their wine was trembling to the beat. They couldn't hear themselves think and went inside and closed the door.

They resumed their conversation in the kitchen.

Liz began to prepare their meal.

"Liz, she's lying."

"John, can we talk about something else?"

"Not until you tell me you believe me."

"All right, I believe you."

"You don't sound too sure."

"John, I believe you. All right? Now, can we talk about something else?"

"Okay. How did the scuba-diving go?"

Liz got some vegetables out of the fridge. "It went very well. I really enjoyed it. I haven't ventured beyond the swimming pool yet, but Sybille said we should go out by the rocks next time."

"Will there *be* a next time?"

Liz ran the cold-water tap. "I don't see why not. I couldn't hope for a better teacher."

"What did you find to talk about for eight hours a day?"

Liz raised an eyebrow. "Eight hours a day? I would have needed institutionalising if I'd had to spend eight hours a day with Sybille."

"So how long was she here?"

"I don't know … two hours a day. Three at the most."

"Then where was she for the rest of the time?"

Chapter 19

One day, when John got back from lunch, Sybille told him the bank had called and left a message for him to please call the manager at his earliest convenience.

"I wonder what he wants," he said.

"If you picked up the phone and called him, you might find out," Sybille said. She walked out into the garden closing the door behind her.

John picked up the phone.

"Thank you for returning my call, John," the bank manager said.

"No problem. What can I do for you, Andy?"

"You're certainly making your mark on the property."

"Have you seen it recently?"

"My wife and I drove out last evening. You have a car park now."

John laughed. "Yes, we do. The painters and decorators started this morning. Come back in a month and you'll really see a difference."

"You'll be starting to advertise them for sale soon, I imagine."

"When the painters and decorators have finished and we've got the new furniture in and the carpets laid. I'm having a sign made, I've already placed the order for that, and I've booked a professional photographer. Then I'll start to advertise them."

From outside there was a leaden thump, followed by a squelching sound and a shriek. And then, "*Jesus Christ*! You almost fucking decapitated me. You moron."

"What on earth was that?" McTavish said.

"That was my charming partner," John said. "It sounds like one of the painters almost decapitated her with a can of paint. She'll have his card marked. What can I do for you, Andy?"

"You need to make another transfer into the company account."

"But I only made one last week. And I haven't cut any cheques since then."

"It's the cash you're taking."

"What cash? The only cash we're taking is the five hundred dollars a week Sybille gets. How much cash are we talking about?"

"Twenty-five thousand dollars."

"I haven't authorised twenty-five thousand dollars in cash, and I would know if Liz had. I think there's been some kind of mistake."

"No mistake, John. We've checked and double-checked. I assumed you were paying some of the contractors in cash."

"I don't pay the contractors in cash. I pay them by cheque."

"And what about your personal account?"

"What about it?"

"Twenty-five thousand dollars has gone from that too."

John could scarcely believe his ears. "Are you telling me that fifty thousand dollars has gone?"

"I'm afraid so."

"What the hell's going on, Andy?"

"I don't know, John. I think you'd better come in, and bring Liz with you. I'll put a stop on your private banking card, and Liz's, and I'll put a stop on the company's debit card. Bring the cards with you and I'll cut them up and issue new ones."

John phoned Liz and gave her a quick rundown on what was going on. He drove straight over and she was waiting outside the apartment for him. He leaned across the vehicle and opened the door for her.

The first thing she said was, "Is it Sybille, do you think?"

"I have no idea," John said. "I sincerely hope not."

At the bank, the manager took the cards and cut them in two. "You'll get new cards within the week," he said. "If you need cash in the meantime, let me know." He slid a couple of computer printouts across his desk. "These are our records of the accounts in question."

Liz moved her chair closer to John's so they could read them together.

The withdrawals had been highlighted. They showed the dates and times of the withdrawals. The first withdrawal from the company account had been made at 09.46 a.m. on the Tuesday of the previous week. The first withdrawal from John's personal account had been made at 4:46 p.m. on the same day. The withdrawals had been made at roughly the same time of day over five consecutive days, making ten withdrawals in all.

"Do the dates mean anything to either of you?"

They did to Liz. "On three of these dates Sybille was giving me scuba diving lessons."

"That's correct," John said. "On three of the dates Sybille was off the property."

"What about the times? Do they jibe with the times she was teaching you to scuba dive, Liz?"

Liz took a closer look. "Actually, no, they don't. Sybille was usually with me between eleven, eleven-thirty in the morning and two, two-thirty in the afternoon."

"I see," the bank manager said. "It's interesting that the amount taken was exactly what she asked me for."

"I can't see it being Sybille," John said, slowly shaking his head. "She might be a lot of things, but stupid she most certainly is not."

"She could be running a double bluff," McTavish suggested.

"She's clever enough," Liz said. "And she knew we had a limit of five thousand dollars a day on cash withdrawals from the company account, because she was with us when we opened the account."

"But she wouldn't have known we had a five thousand dollar limit on our personal account," John said.

"Then if it isn't Sybille, it's probably an inside job," Liz said. "Although Sybille could have an accomplice in the bank."

"I think we can rule that out," McTavish said. "We have stringent checks in place."

"Which isn't to say it doesn't happen sometimes, Andy, with respect," Liz said. "Although I'm not suggesting it happens in this bank."

"Have you fired anyone recently?" John said. "Someone who might have a grudge against the bank?"

"I think you're barking up the wrong tree, John."

"Andy, do you have CCTV on your automatic teller machines?" Liz asked.

"We certainly do. On all of them."

"I assume you've checked the tapes," John said.

"We're doing it as we speak."

"Sybille would know the ATMs are covered by cameras," John said. "And there's the PIN numbers. She wouldn't know the PIN numbers."

"Speaking of which, John," the banker said, "you wouldn't happen to keep a written record of the PIN numbers, would you?"

John looked slightly shame-faced. "I know I shouldn't, but I do. I keep them in my wallet. They are written on the back of one of my old business cards."

"Is the card in your wallet now?"

John got to his feet and unbuttoned the back pocket of his trousers and fished out his wallet. When he saw the business card, his face paled. "Shit! Someone's had their hands on this." He held the card for the others to see. "I keep my cards facing forwards and the right way up. This was facing backwards, and it was upside down."

"Could you be mistaken?" McTavish asked.

Liz answered him. "He won't be mistaken, Andy. The suits and shirts in his wardrobe all face in the same direction. It's a fetish of his. One of his *things*."

"Has your wallet been out of your sight recently, John?"

John scratched his head. "Not that I can remember. Oh, but hang on a second ... yes, it has. I took a swim on the property, and I left ..."

"I didn't know you took your swimming costume to the property," Liz said.

"Sybille lent me a pair. I think they belonged to her son."

"Where was she when you were changing?"

"Knock it off, Liz. Let's not go there again."

"What did you do with your trousers when you took them off?" McTavish asked.

"I hung them over the back of a chair. But that still doesn't mean Sybille took the money."

"No, it doesn't. But I think we have to at least consider her a suspect." The banker's hand hovered over the phone. "I think it's time to bring in the police."

Chapter 20

DCI Richard E Johnson of Freeport CID, a tall broad shouldered Bahamian, walked on to the property with a colleague and asked a painter on a ladder where he might find Sybille Johanssen.

The painter directed him to the office.

Johnson thanked him and then he and his colleague walked to the office, where he rapped sharply on the door.

John was at the far end of the property talking to the painting contractor, but he knew who they were. They were the detectives who had come to the bank after the bank manager had phoned the police about the stolen money. He recalled the two men exchanging knowing looks when Sybille's name was mentioned.

Sybille opened the door. John was too far away to hear what was being said, but he could tell from her body language that she was far from happy. She took a long hard look in his direction, and then stepped back to let the detectives in.

The gardens were looking good again; almost as good as they had been before the renovations had begun. John had had the grass cut before the painters and decorators began, speaking of which, the poor soul who had almost decapitated Sybille with the can of paint was no longer on the property. In fact, he was no longer in the employ of the company. Although he had strenuously denied dropping the can of paint deliberately, and John had believed him, Sybille had not. He had told them, with tears in his eyes that he was a family man with three young children and that, without the job, he would have no means of feeding his family, but while John had been off the property, Sybille had insisted that the contractor not only take him off the job, but actually fire him, threatening to cancel the contract if he didn't.

When the contractor had told John what Sybille had done, he had had words with her, but she had raised such a ruckus about him questioning her decision that he had been forced to let it go.

John had invested in a brand new John Deere ride-on lawn mower with a forty-two inch cutting deck which, when not in use, languished in a wooden shed he had had built for the purpose. To Henry, the gardener, this was his Christmases all coming together at once, and there had been tears in his eyes when John had handed him the key to the gleaming machine.

It was time to be thinking about getting a sign made and John had seen one he liked on an apartment complex on the outskirts of Freeport. He had talked to the owner of the property, and the man, who had designed the sign himself, had been so flattered by the praise John had heaped on the sign, that he had been only too pleased to tell John who had made it for him.

John had gone to the factory and ordered an identical sign. It was a wooden, white-painted sign with the name, telephone number and fax number painted in black gloss. The sign stood five feet high and five feet wide. It was the type of sign that is concreted to the ground. The sign was costing almost a thousand dollars, but John knew it would be worth every cent in helping give an excellent first impression of the property.

He wanted to have a word with the detectives, who had still not emerged from the office, and he wandered round the property before finally ending up at the car park.

There were five vehicles in the car park: a small flat-bed truck and two vans, all bearing the name and logo of the painting contractor, his own Grand Cherokee, and a bog-standard black saloon car, which he took to be the car in which the detectives had come.

The weeds were long gone, but there was considerable damage to the concrete from where they had been pulled out. Representatives from two Tarmac companies were coming in to see him later in the week, to give him a quote on resurfacing the car park, and he had agreed a date with a landscape gardener to talk about landscaping the area.

There was still no sign of the detectives and it was far too hot to be standing out in the sun without a hat, so John walked over to the beach, found a tree from where he could see the detectives' car, and sat down.

When they finally emerged, the detectives had been with Sybille over an hour and a half.

John got to his feet, brushed the sand off his trousers and caught up with them as they reached their car.

"We don't think she had anything to do with it," Johnson said.

"Neither do I," John said. "Did she say where she was when she was supposed to be giving my wife scuba diving lessons?"

"She told us it was none of our business where she was. By the way, I should warn you that she's hopping mad."

When John got to the office, Sybille was standing in the doorway with the door open. She beckoned him with her finger. He followed her in.

Sybille had a liking for fresh flowers, which she displayed in a rather nice cut-glass vase on the coffee table. She picked the vase up and hurled it at the wall at the far end of the room. The vase shattered, leaving chunks of glass and cut flowers all over the floor and streams of water running down the wall.

Sybille paced the room, her chest heaving. And then she stopped pacing and stood facing him, her face inches from his. "How *dare* you accuse me of stealing?" Her voice was controlled, but he knew she was seething. It was like looking into the eyes of a lioness with starving cubs.

To try and defuse the situation, John stepped back a couple of paces and then sat down, leaving Sybille standing over him. "I didn't accuse you of stealing, Sybille," he said quietly. "And I wasn't the one who called in the police. I never thought you had anything to do with it, and I still don't."

"Why don't I believe you? You bastard!"

"The police had to do what they had to do, which was eliminate you from their enquiries. And for your information,

Sybille, and I probably shouldn't be telling you this, they don't think you had anything to do with it, either."

"I didn't take your fucking money."

"I know you didn't."

"It's that fucking wife of yours, isn't it? She's had it in for me from the start."

"She hasn't, Sybille. I won't deny that ..."

"I've had it with the fucking pair of you. Let's get this fucking place finished and then I can get you the hell out of my life."

Chapter 21

Sybille had had two effigies made: one of John, in a dark blue blazer, white shirt and grey trousers, and one of Liz, in a print dress with a flared skirt. Their faces had been painted on, and the detail was surprisingly good.

Sybille was making a feature of them, as if they were part of the furniture. She had stood them on a tall slim table she had probably bought for a few dollars in the Straw Market, and she had positioned the table against the wall, roughly where she had thrown the vase. Anyone walking into the office would see them immediately.

A red satin pin cushion sat between the effigies. In it were stuck ten pins; five with blue heads and five with pink heads.

John picked up the effigy of him. He was studying its workmanship when Sybille walked in.

"What do you think?" she asked amiably.

"Of what? The workmanship, or the fact that you've made them?"

"Had them made," Sybille said. "I don't make them myself. I meant the workmanship; what do you think of the workmanship?"

"The workmanship is excellent. Who makes them for you?"

"If I told you that I'd have to kill you."

John laughed. "Very impressive. As a matter of interest, Sybille, how many of these have you had made?"

"I don't remember exactly. A few."

"I assume blue for me and pink for Liz."

"No flies on you, then."

"And whoever pisses you off gets a pin in their effigy, right?"

"You're getting the drift."

"When do they get buried in the seabed?"

"Need you ask? Five pins; go figure. Speaking of which, I owe you both a pin for calling in the police. Will you do the honours, or shall I?"

"I'll do it," John said. "I'd like to see if it hurts when you stick a pin in it." He took a pin with a blue head from the pin cushion. "Where shall I stick it?"

"It doesn't matter where you stick it. As long as it isn't going to fall out."

John stuck the pin through the chest of his effigy. "Damn," he said, "I didn't feel a thing. How very disappointing."

"You won't be joking when you have five of them in you. One down, four to go."

The exterior walls and woodwork had all been painted and the decorators were working on the interiors of the apartments. Sybille had come up with the idea of using brass numbers on the apartment doors, and the combination of brass on black gloss was very effective. It added a certain elegance. The shingles being reddish in colour, the roofs almost made the buildings look like they were wearing Easter bonnets. The only thing dating the buildings now was the style of their construction. Otherwise they looked as if they had just been built.

The sign stood firmly concreted into the ground by the entrance to the car park. It made a serious statement and John was very pleased with it. The car park had been resurfaced and white lines had been painted to create parking spaces, and the landscape gardener was starting work the day after tomorrow. In the apartments themselves, the new carpets would be laid once the paint had dried, and then the new furniture would be installed. John had booked a photographer and he was now starting to get his head around how he would market the apartments.

John was sitting in the office having a quiet coffee with Sybille one day when four people, two men and two women, wandered on to the property from the direction of the car park. He went out to see what they wanted.

"Can I help you?" he said.

"You the proprietor?" one of the men said.

"Yes, I'm the proprietor. John McLaren. How can I help you?"

The man offered his hand. "Hi, I'm Greg."

He sounded Canadian.

"Nice to meet you, Greg."

"You too. Place is looking good."

"Thank you. It's almost finished now."

"What will you do with it when it's finished?"

"The plan is to sell the apartments. They'll be on the market shortly. Are you interested in buying one?"

"What do you reckon they're worth?"

"I'll be looking for forty thousand dollars. Do you want to see one while you're here? They're nice apartments, fully air-conditioned, and ..."

"Nah, don't think so. Well nice talking with you, John. You have a good day."

They walked off in the direction of the car park leaving John standing there scratching his head.

"What did they want?" Sybille said.

"I haven't a clue. That was extraordinary. I have no idea why they came."

"Did they want to buy an apartment?"

"No, I offered to show them one, but they weren't interested."

"I have a vague feeling I've seen those of the guys before," Sybille said. "The one you shook hands with."

The phone rang. Sybille answered it. She passed the phone to John. "It's your detective friend."

"We found out who took the money," DCI Johnson said. "I won't go into detail on the phone, but you'll be getting a call from your bank. I thought I'd like to tell you myself."

"What did *he* want?" Sybille said.

"They've found out who took the money."

"So, do you believe me now?"

"Sybille, I never doubted you."

Ten minutes later the bank manager phoned to say they had found out who had taken the money and that the bank would be replacing the money.

"Who was it, Andy?"

"One of our employees. So much for me saying it couldn't happen."

When John gave Liz the news that evening, her eyes twinkled. "So you *did* put the card in your wallet upside down and back to front. Well fancy that. You are human, after all."

Chapter 22

John was standing at the balcony rail watching a three-masted schooner turn into the channel. It was one of those luxuriously appointed vessels well-heeled corporations use for entertaining purposes. Its sails had been furled and it was entering the channel under power. Its name was *Fancy Free*. It looked too wide to get into the channel, but it made it with room to spare.

And speaking of boats, the boat he had ordered should have been delivered by now. But no sweat, the time for messing around on boats was after the apartments had been sold.

They had eaten breakfast on the balcony and Liz was making him a coffee before he went off to the property.

The phone rang. Liz answered it. "It's Nicholas," she said, handing him the phone.

"Good morning, Nicholas."

"Are you sitting down?"

"Should I be?"

"It might be better if you were."

John sat down. "Okay, I'm sitting down."

"I'm not sure how to put this …"

"I'm a big boy, Nicholas. Spit out."

"You can't sell the apartments."

"Who says we can't?"

"A High Court judge."

"What does a High Court judge have to do with anything?"

"Quite a lot, as it happens. John, let me explain. A former partner of Enrico's is claiming he lent Enrico money, and Enrico promised to pay him back if he ever sold the property.

The individual in question has just been over for a vacation and he's seen what you've done with the place. Now he wants his money back."

"Would his name happen to be Greg? And would he happen to be Canadian?"

"Yes, and yes. His name's Greg Elkington. How did you know?"

John explained about the visitors. "Now I wish I'd kept my big mouth shut. How much money are we talking about?"

"I understand from his solicitor that he hasn't mentioned a figure."

"Odd that, isn't it? Wouldn't you have thought that if you'd lent money to someone, you would know how much you'd lent him?"

"My sentiments exactly. Which is why I think he may be trying it on."

"As if we didn't have enough to worry about. Are you saying there might never have been a loan?"

"It's entirely possible, John. Stranger things have happened."

John was lost for words.

"John, look …"

"Is there paperwork to support his claim?"

"No, there isn't. And I have all of Enrico's files. I'll fight it, of course. But these things can drag on."

"Do you think it might help if I met the guy?"

"With a view to what?"

"Strangling him, perhaps."

"I'll pretend I didn't hear that."

"I could make him an offer."

"Since it's got to the stage where lawyers and High Court judges are involved, I think it would be better if you let me handle this."

"Does Sybille know?"

"Yes, she knows."

"How did she take it?"

"You know Sybille."

"All right, Nicholas. Thank you for letting me know."

Liz had been listening to John's side of the conversation. She asked him what was going on.

He brought her up to speed. And then he said, "I need to talk this over with Sybille, and I'd like you to come with me. Three heads may be better than two in a situation like this."

Liz had not been to the property for some considerable time, and when she saw what had been done, her mouth fell open. "My God! Can this really be the same place?"

The landscape gardener was laying black plastic sheeting between the shrubs, bushes, cacti and ornamental trees he had planted. He was then covering the plastic with pine bark.

John had found a wholesaler with five thousand square feet of good quality carpet he was anxious to dispose of, and John had taken it off his hands at a knockdown price. Two carpet fitters were kneeling on the lawn outside the office cutting lengths off full-width rolls.

Liz spotted the effigies as soon as she walked into the office. She knew about them, because John had told her, but although her brow darkened, she didn't say a word.

Sybille was banging around in the kitchen muttering, "Where am I going to get a fucking job at my age?"

"You won't need to look for a job, Sybille," John said from the kitchen doorway. "We'll find a way. Come on, let's sit down and talk this through. Liz is here."

Sybille calmed down and made coffee.

The apartment looked good. It had been decorated and carpet had been laid. The place smelt strongly of paint and new carpet, but John was pleased. The old furniture was still in situ, but they all knew where to sit to avoid the lumps.

"It's hard to believe the guy can get away with this," John said, to kick things off. "The judicial system in the Bahamas is supposed to be based on the British system, but this feels more like we're living in a Banana Republic. How can a High Court judge rule in favour of someone who has no evidence whatsoever to prove that a loan was ever made? It's bordering on insanity."

"We're screwed," Sybille said. "Aren't we? We're well and truly screwed."

"Not necessarily," John said. "Let's look at the facts. What we can't do is sell the apartments. We have no way of knowing when the injunction will be lifted, but no one has said anything about us not being able to rent them out."

Sybille pulled a face. "I'm not sure that's such a good idea. Can you imagine trying to get rid of a whole load of sitting tenants when the injunction's lifted?"

"That's not what I had in mind," John said. "What I had in mind is to run the place as a condominium hotel."

Sybille perked up visibly. "I never thought of that. A friend of mine runs a condominium hotel."

"What's a condominium hotel?" Liz asked.

"It's an all suites hotel, Liz," John said. "Like that neighbour of ours in Orlando had."

"Joe?"

"Yes, Joe. Joe and Cathy."

"But we don't have a restaurant."

"Neither did they."

"It's self-catering," Sybille explained. "Guests would cook their food themselves. It's perfect. They'll have a fit when they see what food costs over here."

"But offset against that," John said, "is that they'll be paying a lot less for their accommodation than if they were staying in a hotel. From what I've seen, I reckon we could get thirty dollars a night, per unit, and if we could achieve that, I think it would be viable."

Sybille had worked the figures out in her head as John had been talking. "That would give us twelve hundred dollars a night."

"But that would be based on full occupancy, which we couldn't hope to achieve immediately, if ever. And there would be costs, such as a couple of chambermaids and a receptionist. But you would know more about that than I would."

"Who do you have in mind to run the hotel?" Sybille asked.

"How about you?" John said. "I handle the marketing, you run the hotel."

"I'm not sure about that," Sybille said. "I've only just got rid of the last lot."

Liz almost blew a gasket. "If by *the last lot* you are referring to those unfortunate people dying of cancer, you should be ashamed of yourself. How dare you refer to them as *the last lot*? And while I'm on the subject, I've heard about the disgusting state of the bedding you had them sleeping in. If you think you can run our hotel under conditions like that, you'd better think again."

Sybille stared at her for a moment or two, and then she enquired amiably, "Have you finished?"

"I could go on," Liz said. "For some time, as it happens, but this is neither the time nor the place. So for the moment, yes, I'm finished."

"Good, then I have a present for you." Sybille got to her feet and marched across the room and picked up Liz's effigy and a pink pin. "Now, let's see. Where shall I stick it?"

"For heaven's sake, Sybille, grow up," Liz said irritably. "Stick it wherever you like."

Chapter 23

Liz was rising and falling with the swell of the ocean. She was face down watching a southern spotted ray cruising along the seabed some twenty feet below. The tips of its wings were puffing up little spurts of sand. Liz was working her fins just enough to keep up with it.

Something touched her shoulder. She struggled to an upright position and yanked the snorkel out of her mouth. "You idiot!" she said, her heart pounding. "I thought it was a shark. I thought my end had come."

"Sorry to disappoint you," John said, grinning.

"What are you doing here? You're supposed to be on the property."

"I have some news for you."

They trod water, rising and falling with the swell.

"John, unless it's good news, I don't want to hear it. I've had enough of the other kind to last me a lifetime."

"Let's get out of the water. Race you to the beach."

John was an excellent swimmer, winning medals at school, but Liz was wearing fins and she easily outpaced him. She slowed down as they approached the beach, so the race would end up a draw. She took off her snorkelling gear and they walked out of the water together, laughing.

Liz had left her towel on the beach and they sat on it to let the sun dry them. John had been so enthusiastic to tell Liz about the decision he had made that he had forgotten to bring a towel with him.

Liz ran her fingers through her wet hair. "So, what was so important you almost caused me to die of a heart attack?"

"Before I tell you," John said, "let me ask you a question. Do you like living here?"

Liz eyed him suspiciously. "That sounds like a loaded question if ever I heard one. Where's this leading?"

"Humour me for a moment, Liz, please. Do you enjoy living here?"

Liz scratched her knee, as if this would help her think. "I suppose the best way I can answer that is to say that I do, and I don't. As to the do's, some things I like very much."

"Such as?"

"Such as the apartment, being able to swim and fish and snorkel whenever I feel like it. I like the golf, not that we've had the opportunity to play many of the courses. And I especially like some of the people we've met here. People like Rolly, George, Jill. A few others."

She paused.

"But?" John said.

"I hate being on my own all the time. If you didn't come home in the evenings it would be like it was when you were away on business back in England before you retired. And I hate that you spend so much time with Sybille. It's not you I don't trust, it's her."

"How would you feel about going back to Florida?"

"Don't joke about things like that, John. You know perfectly well that I would give my eye teeth to go back to Florida. But we can't, can we?"

"I think we can. In fact, I think we should."

"But what about the property?"

"Liz, let me explain."

Liz drew up her knees, wrapped her arms round her legs, rested her chin on her knees and gave him her full attention.

John scooped up some sand and let it run through his fingers as he thought how best to put across what he had to say. And then he began to explain that he had come to the conclusion that the best place from which to market the property as a condo hotel would be Orlando, where major travel agents, tours operators, airlines and shipping lines operated from. "I think that if I tried to do it from here I'd be hopping on planes to Orlando every five minutes, and US Immigration wouldn't be too happy about that."

"But if we went back to Florida, John, wouldn't we be in the same situation with our visas as before?"

"Well," John said, scooping up more sand and letting it run through his fingers, "our visas will get us six months, as they did before, but this time I'll get something more permanent organised. Last time, I was so wrapped up in finding myself a business that I took my eye off the ball. I won't let that happen again."

"Have you discussed this with Sybille?"

"Not yet. I wanted to talk to you first."

"How do you think she'll react?"

"I don't know. And quite frankly, Liz, I don't much care.

A sport fishing boat motored down the channel and, as it got closer, they could see it was George Humphries' boat, *Catch Me If You Can*. Humphries was at the wheel on the upper deck and Jill was in the fishing chair on the lower deck, with her feet on the rail and her sunglasses in her hair.

All four of them waved.

"Hi, guys," Humphries called.

"Hi, Jill," Liz called. "Hi, George."

"When are we getting together again?" John called.

"Soon." Humphries put his hand to his ear to indicate he would call him.

Liz and Jill blew kisses to each other.

The stern sat down and they roared off into the distance.

"Jill's become a real friend to you, hasn't she?" John said.

"She's been my rock," Liz said. "I don't know what I would have done without her."

"Has it been so bad?"

"I don't really want to talk about it."

"Why didn't you talk to me when you had a problem?"

"You had enough on your plate."

John put his arm round her shoulders. "Darling, I'm so sorry."

Her eyes began to fill up. "Don't be nice to me," she said. "You'll only make me cry."

When John got to the property the next morning there were offcuts of new carpet all over the lawn.

Sybille was sitting in a deckchair by the pool.

"Good morning, Sybille."

Sybille scowled. "Where the hell were you yesterday afternoon?"

"I don't think I need to account to you for my movements. But, since you asked, I was playing golf with Liz."

"It's all right for some," Sybille said sourly.

There was another deckchair nearby. John dragged it over and sat beside her.

Two carpet fitters emerged from one of the ground floor apartments. They were struggling with a large piece of the old carpet. They were trying to get it through the door and they hadn't seemed to realise that if they had rolled the carpet up, it would have gone through the door with ease.

"Fucking Bahamians," Sybille muttered. "They haven't a fucking clue. Hey!" she yelled.

Neither man looked. They had either not heard her, or they were ignoring her.

John suspected the latter.

"Hey, you two! Listen to me when I'm talking to you!"

The men stopped struggling with the carpet and looked over.

"You watch my new paintwork. Okay? Otherwise you'll be getting a bill."

The men looked at each other, muttered something, sniggered, and got back to struggling with the carpet.

It was so rare for John to see people not letting a tongue-lashing from Sybille bother them that John had to smile.

"What are you looking so fucking pleased about?"

"Sybille, there are other words in the English language. Must you use the f-word every time you open your mouth?"

Sybille glared at him, but said nothing.

John was having serious doubts as to whether this was a good time to be giving Sybille his news. But then she was so rarely in anything other than a bad mood these days that there might never be a good time. He decided to go for it. "Liz and I are going back to Florida."

"Well bully for you. How long are you going for?"

He realised she had misunderstood him. "No, we're going back permanently. I'm going to market the property from Orlando."

"And what am I supposed to do?"

"Well, I was sort of hoping, Sybille, that you would run the property, as you promised to do. But if you've changed your mind, I can always ..."

"That was when I thought you would be here with me. What happens when I need to talk to you?"

"You pick up the phone."

"How do we pay the bills?"

"You fax me the invoice, and I'll Fed Ex you a cheque. You'll get it the next day."

"When will I see you?"

"Probably not very often."

"What about when we need to meet?"

"You can take a day trip to Orlando. It will be a break from the property for you."

"You've got it all worked out, haven't you? Leaving me to do all the work. You'll be getting another pin in your effigy for this."

"Sybille, you can stick as many pins in my effigy as you like. It will be worth it to get away from you."

"When are you leaving?'

"As soon as I can get things organised."

"Good. The sooner the better."

Chapter 24

The phone in the apartment rang one morning before John had left for the property and the hairs on his neck stood up when he realised who was calling.

"Your boat's arrived," the boat dealer said. "Customs and Excise have it in their bonded warehouse. I'll pay the duty, then they'll release the boat to me and I'll fit it out."

Christ Almighty! What kind of timing was this? He had just taken the decision to go back to Florida, and the bloody boat arrives. What the hell was he to do with an ocean-going boat equipped with satellite navigation and ship-to-shore radio in Orlando? He needed time to think.

"How long will it take to fit it out?"

"Two weeks, give or take."

"Okay, call when it's ready."

The only thing John could think of was to sell the boat. But did he sell it here, or sell it in Florida? The idea of taking it back to Florida seemed ludicrous. He was sure of one thing; wherever he sold it, he would lose money on it.

He was in the office thinking about it, and Sybille caught his mood.

"Something wrong, John?"

"My boat's arrived."

"I would have thought most people about to take possession of their first boat would be jumping for joy, not sitting there with a face like a wet weekend."

"The problem is; I'll be living in Orlando where the only patch of water of any note is a bass fishing lake."

"I don't understand. You'll have the Atlantic Ocean on one side and the Gulf of Mexico on the other. You won't be short of water."

"But they are an hour's drive from Orlando, and I know what would happen: the boat would sit on its trailer and never get used."

"So what are you going to do with it?"

"I'm going to do the only thing I can do; I'm going to sell it."

Sybille's ears pricked up. "Remind me what kind of boat it is."

John gave her a rundown on the boat.

"What price will you be looking for?"

"I haven't worked it out, yet. But I've put forty-two thousand dollars into it, so I'll be wanting something close."

"I'd like to take a look at it."

"With a view to what?"

"With a view to buying it. Why else would I want to take a look at it?"

"Don't think me rude, Sybille, but where would you get forty-two thousand dollars?"

"You're not the only one with imagination round here, John. When we start making a profit on this place, half of it will be mine. Right?"

"Right."

"And you have confidence in your ability to get heads in beds when you get to Orlando. Right?"

"Right."

"Then, if you're prepared to let me have the boat on extended terms, I'll start paying for it when we start turning a profit."

John could not fault her logic, and he knew he would never find an easier solution to his problem. "When would you like to see it?" he said.

The boat, which was standing on its trailer in the dealer's yard, gleamed like a new pin. It had not yet been fully fitted out, although the outboard motor had been fitted. The hull was cream, with brown trim. The chromium-plated bow rail and tee-tops supports shone like mirrors.

"Very smart," Sybille said. "I like the colour scheme." She wasted no time in clambering aboard and making a beeline for the stern, where she seemed inordinately interested in the outboard motor.

John stood with the dealer, watching her. John had acquainted the dealer with the fact that he wanted to sell the boat and that he would be bringing his business partner to take a look at it.

Sybille finally spoke. "Would there be room for a second engine?"

The dealer stepped back and took a long hard look at the transom. Finally, he nodded. "Yes, I think there's room for a second engine. Although you would lose the swimming platform."

"I'm not interested in a swimming platform," Sybille said.

"Do you want me to get you a price?"

"What speed would she do with two engines?"

"I couldn't say exactly ... fifty, fifty-five knots at a guess. Maybe sixty, with a following wind." He smiled at his own joke.

Sybille walked to the centre console.

They walked by the side of the boat, keeping pace with her.

Sybille leaned on the leaning post and toyed with the steering wheel. "John told me she has satellite navigation, ship-to-shore radio, and depth gauge."

"That's correct," the dealer said. "Let me show you where they are." He climbed aboard.

Sybille let him show her where everything was, and how it all worked. And then she said, "What if I wanted radar?'

John now knew beyond a shadow of a doubt why Sybille was interested in his boat. But if she wanted to buy his boat to run drugs, it was not his concern. He would be off the island and she would be shown on the paperwork as the legal owner of the boat; he would make sure of that. There could be no comeback on him, he was merely selling her a boat.

"Sure," the dealer said. "I can fit radar."

"And spotlights?"

"I'll light her up like a Christmas tree for you if you like."

"What about storage?"

"There are fish boxes, and there's deep storage under the seats. Let me show you."

Sybille let him show her all the storage the boat had to offer, which was considerable, and then she walked to the bow and stood with her hands on the rail, as if looking out to sea. Finally, she said, "Let me think about it."

As they were leaving his premises, the dealer took John to one side. "If she doesn't buy it, I'll sell it for you. At a commission, of course."

John leaned in close. "Let me tell you something, *fella*," he hissed. "After the way you shafted me when I bought the boat, I would rather give the bloody thing to charity."

"There would need to be paperwork, Sybille," John said in the Grand Cherokee on the way back to the property. "It's a lot of money we're talking about."

"I'll have Nicky draw up an agreement."

"Does that mean you're interested?"

"I'm very interested, John. In fact, I'll take it."

"Since I'll be giving you extended terms, Sybille, it will have to be at the full price."

"I have no problem with that."

"When you speak to Nicholas, tell him to include a clause to facilitate ownership reverting to me, in the event you default on payment."

"I will. But I won't, if you get my drift." She grinned.

John looked at her sternly. "Sybille, be warned that I *will* repossess the boat if you don't make the payments. Okay?"

Sybille patted his knee. "You won't need to repossess it, John. Trust me on this."

Chapter 25

With the move back to Florida pending, John had much to do.

One thing he needed to do was talk his way out of the remaining three months on the rental agreement on the apartment, and he thought the best way to achieve this would be to invite Rolly Schaerer round for a drink one evening.

"No problem," Schaerer said, after John had explained the situation to him. "Pay me until the day you leave, and we'll call it quits."

"That calls for a glass or three of my eighteen-year-old Macallan," John said, getting to his feet.

"Oh, God, not that awful stuff again. I still have a headache from the last time." Schaerer grinned.

"Well someone has to drink it," John said. "We can't have the distillery going out of business."

"Hell, no!"

"What can I get you, darling?"

"I'll have a glass of Chardonnay, John. There's a bottle open in the fridge."

"Are you and Sybille still an item, Rolly?" Liz said, as John went off to get the drinks organised. "I don't remember seeing her vehicle round here recently."

Schaerer shook his head. "She moved on. We haven't been an item for some time."

"I'm sorry. I didn't know."

"Don't be. I'm glad to be rid of her."

John's bottle of eighteen-year-old Macallan was a smidgeon over half full. He unscrewed the top and threw it in the wastepaper basket. "Now we're here until the bottle's empty," he said.

"I'll drink to that," Schaerer said, his eyes feasting on the triple John was pouring him. "When," he said, indicating John should stop pouring. "I think."

John grinned and poured him a drop more.

The three of them touched glasses.

"Cheers."

Schaerer took a swallow and rolled his eyes. "Boy! Is that good, or is that good?"

They got on to the subject of what John was going to do with his vehicle and Schaerer offered to take it off his hands if he was thinking of selling it. "I've always like the Grand Cherokee, and I've been thinking of getting a new vehicle."

John had been giving the subject of what to do with the vehicle some considerable thought. Like the boat, it had come from Florida, and, like the boat, he had paid an inordinate amount of Bahamian import duty on it. Shipping it back to Florida made no economic sense whatsoever.

"You could use it until the day you left," Schaerer continued, "and I'll even drive you to the airport in it. What do you say?"

"I say, my friend, that once we agree a price you have yourself a deal."

They shook hands on a deal two minutes later.

Their glasses were getting dangerously low and John poured a couple more triples. Liz said no to a third glass of wine.

The subject of John's boat came up and Schaerer was aghast when John told him he had cut a deal with Sybille. "I hope you know what you're doing. I wouldn't trust her further than I could kick her, now."

"What do you mean by *now*, Rolly?" Liz enquired.

"I mean now I've learned more about her."

"Would you care to elucidate?" John said.

"Sure. First off, are you aware she's involved in running drugs?"

"Yes, we knew that much," John said.

Schaerer took another slurp of scotch. "Second off, she's obsessed with money. She'll do whatever it takes to get her hands on it. And third off, and I've been meaning to tell you this, is that she told me she would own the property herself one day. And she's the kind of woman who will stop at nothing until she achieves her goal."

The next thing John needed to do was get a flier organised. Since he couldn't take the tourism industry in Orlando to the property, he would have to take the property to them.

His flier would need to contain details of the property and also details of the many and varied facilities Grand Bahama had to offer, in addition to the obligatory sand, sea and sun, and he figured that the man to help him put this together was the photographer, with whom he had spoken on the telephone on a number of occasions but had never actually met. He phoned him and told him what he was looking for. It just so happened that the photographer had considerable expertise in the field of fliers and, when he came to the property to take photographs, he brought with him scores of photographs he had taken of the island's facilities with him. This was manna from heaven for John, because it meant he did not have to go digging for photographs himself.

The photographer took dozens of photographs of the property, both inside and out, the gardens, the swimming pool and the beach. He even suggested an aerial shot to show the proximity of the property to the Atlantic Ocean. But this would have meant hiring a helicopter and John baulked at this. John also wanted 10 x 8 glossies of the property, to show the industry, and he also needed a schematic plan of an apartment interior. He wanted to be in a position to sit across someone's desk and hand over a business card, flier, photographs, and a plan showing the layout of an apartment, he himself providing a verbal commentary.

Then bingo! They would be flocking to buy. Yeah, right! If only it was that simple. He was under no illusions as to how hard he was going to have to work to get hard-bitten industry executives interested in the property. Years of experience of international marketing in a previous life had taught him that much.

While he waited for the photographs to be developed, John visited the island's golf courses. These were all pay-and-play courses, meaning anyone could turn up and play, and at most of the courses clubs could be hired, sometimes shoes even. He collected maps of the courses, score cards and details of green fees, cart hire, etc.

With the photographs to hand, John sat down with the photographer to decide on which pictures to use. He had already prepared the text. The photographer then took John to a printer friend who specialised in fliers and John was amazed, and delighted, by how little the fliers were going to cost him. It was difficult to estimate the number he would need, because he was sailing in uncharted waters, but as the fliers were only costing eighteen cents each, he ordered five thousand.

The photographer's bill was a whole other ball game. It almost made John's eyes water. But he had got what he wanted, and at considerably less than he had expected.

And last, but certainly not least, they couldn't leave the island without doing something for George and Jill Humphries. Not only had the Humphries welcomed them with open arms when they had arrived on the island, they had shown them the restaurants, got them invitations to parties, and even taken them tuna fishing. Liz and Jill had been virtual soul mates since day one, and John now regarded George as his best friend, occasionally phoning him for advice when he was having a particular problem with Sybille.

They took the Humphries to dinner at Lucianos' at Port Lucaya and George insisted on buying Champagne. "To celebrate getting rid of two very tiresome people," he said, with a chuckle. This was to be the beginning of a riotous evening ending as dawn was breaking. Humphries' parting shot was, "It's only a fifty minute flight, guys. So don't be strangers. Okay?"

John's liver ached for a week.

Chapter 26

When people travel between the Bahamas and the United States, they pass through US immigration at their port of departure, which, in the case of John and Liz, was Freeport airport.

The immigration officer looked bored out of his skull. He put out his hand. "Passports."

John had tucked the completed immigration forms in their passports. He handed over the passports.

The immigration officer extracted the forms, and then flicked through the passports until he found the page on which their visas – in their case B1/B2 Business visas – were stamped. He started entering the information into his computer. "What's the purpose of your visit?" He sounded so disinterested that John wondered why he didn't look for a more interesting job. He was reminded of the old joke: If you pay people peanuts, what do you get? The answer: monkeys.

John explained about the property and his plans for it.

"The last time you lived in the United States, you overstayed your welcome."

Here we go. "Yes, I'm sorry about that. It was an oversight on my part. It won't happen again."

"Will you be employing Americans in the United States?"

"Not directly, but we will be giving American companies the opportunity to make money out of our property. So, indirectly, yes, we will."

"Will you be investing money in the United States?"

The immigration officer was asking his questions as if by rote; as if he didn't give a damn about the answers.

"Not until the property is making a profit. But then I'm sure we shall."

The immigration officer picked up his rubber stamp. He slammed it on his inkpad and banged it on John's passport. He repeated the procedure with Liz's passport. He handed the passports to John. "*Next!*"

When their plane landed at the Orlando International Airport, Liz was so glad to be back that she knelt down and kissed the ground.

John leased a car and they spent the next couple of days looking for somewhere to live. They found a furnished two-bedroom apartment overlooking a lake midway between downtown Orlando and Walt Disney World. It was on the first floor of the building and was accessed by a wide flight of wooden stairs from the car park. It was the rent that clinched it; John felt the need to be circumspect with money until the property started turning a profit.

The real estate broker showed them on to the decking at the rear of the apartment. "Two alligators live in the lake," she said. "You see them on the bank sometimes, basking in the sun."

Liz took John to one side. "Let's take it," she said. "We'll find something better when we're making a profit."

They signed a six-month rental agreement and moved in the next day.

John found an office in a full-service office building on Sand Lake Road, a ten-minute drive from the apartment. The room was on the top floor of the building, facing south. From his blue-tinted window he could see the roof of the Shamu Stadium at Sea World, and the golf-ball shaped dome of Spaceship Earth at Walt Disney World's Epcot Center some distance away. The receptionist recommended a printer specialising in high quality business cards.

Now he had addresses, John phoned George Humphries. He had his modular desk, filing cabinet and computer delivered directly to the office. He then bought a fax machine, which doubled as a photocopier.

Then he phoned Sybille.

"Oh, it's you," Sybille said. "Aren't you the guy who was supposed to be keeping in touch? Where the hell have you been?"

John did not rise to the bait. "Finding somewhere to live, finding myself an office and getting business cards printed. If you have a pencil, I'll give you my office address and phone number." He gave her the details and asked how things were at her end.

"They're fine. Apart from waiting for you to get your ass in gear, I've got a receptionist lined up, and two chambermaids on standby. And I've found where I can get good quality bedding and towels at very competitive prices."

"Good. Have you been out on the boat yet?'

"Several times. She goes like shit off a shovel. I've named her Sybille One."

"What do you mean, you've *named her*? I hope that doesn't mean you've had your name painted on the boat."

"Is it a problem?"

"Sybille, that's *my* boat until you've made the final payment on it."

"Well pardon me for living, I'm sure. What do you want me to do, paint it out?"

John had better things to do. "Forget it, it's not important."

John went to his office every day and started compiling a list of wholesalers, travel agents, tour operators, cruise lines and airlines operating in the area. When it was complete, the list ran to three foolscap pages. And then he began phoning people.

It soon became evident that this was not going to work, since, firstly, people simply asked him questions about the property which meant he never got to show them his photographs and the layout of the apartments, and, secondly, because most of them had already made commitments for the season.

So he started dropping in on people, unannounced. No one seemed to mind him dropping in without an appointment, which meant he was at least able to give them his business card and show them his material, but it was the same old problem: they had already made commitments.

John was nothing, if not tenacious, and, spurred on by having forty-two furnished apartments lying idle and his capital being depleted at the rate of eight thousand dollars a month – four thousand dollars to Enrico Rodrigues and four thousand to Sybille – he ploughed on. His luck changed the day he walked into the reception area of Harry Cook Inc, a travel wholesaler with offices on International Drive.

The receptionist, Janice – according to the badge pinned to her blouse – smiled at him. "Good morning, sir. How may I help you?"

"Good morning, I'm John McLaren. Would it be possible to speak with Mr Cook?" He handed her his business card. His card showed him to be the proprietor of the property.

Janice read his card. "Do you have an appointment, John?"

"I'm afraid not, Janice. I dropped in on the off-chance."

"Harry doesn't usually see people without an appointment, but, with an accent like yours, we can't let a little thing like that get in the way. Let me see what I can do." She picked up the phone. "Harry, there's a gentleman from England in reception. He's the proprietor of a property on Grand Bahama and he's asking to see you." She listened for a moment or two, said, "Right," and then put the phone down. "This might be your lucky day, John. He'll be right out."

A slim ginger-haired man in his mid-to-late thirties appeared and Janice handed him John's business card. The man studied the card. "So, you have a property on Grand Bahama."

"Yes, I have."

Cook put out his hand. "I'm Harry Cook."

"John McLaren."

They shook hands.

Cook was casualness personified. He wore a white T-shirt bearing the legend *Nothing But The Best*, faded jeans and tasselled loafers.

John, who was wearing a suit and tie, felt distinctly overdressed.

"Come on through. I want to hear about this property of yours." Cook led the way into a conference room, where he walked to the far end of a long table and sat down. He gestured to the chair beside him.

John sat down and put his briefcase on his lap and opened it. In it were a tourist map of the island, with the property marked with a felt-tipped X; the 10 x 8 glossy photographs of the property, gardens, swimming pool and beach; fifty or sixty fliers, and all the information John had collected about the golf courses. Whatever else he needed was in his head.

"Right," Cook said. "Shoot."

John handed him the photographs. "There are forty-two one-bedroom apartments and they sleep four; two in the bedroom and two on the sofa bed in the living room."

Cook listened to John's commentary as he studied the photographs. He took his time. "Are the apartments air-conditioned?"

"Yes, they're fully air-conditioned. And they're brand new units."

"The furniture looks new."

"It is; it's brand new. It's only just been delivered."

Cook looked up. "I like your enthusiasm, John. You're obviously passionate about your property."

"I'm very passionate about it. I have a lot riding on it. I went out on a limb with this."

"Good man. That means you're committed to it." Cook put the photographs down. "It looks very nice, John, very nice indeed. Where is it located on the island?"

John handed him the tourist map and pointed to the X. "Right there."

"Being on a beach is a big plus."

"And it's virtually our own beach. There are no other properties in the immediate vicinity, and the beach is usually deserted."

Cook scratched his head. "We do a lot business in the Bahamas, and I can't understand why I don't already know about this property."

"Because it's never been on the market before. Well, not as a condo hotel."

"What's your rack rate?"

"Thirty dollars a night."

"Is that per apartment, or per person?"

"Per apartment."

"I think you've got that about right."

"I need to net thirty dollars, so if you offer them at thirty-five dollars I'll cut you in for a five-dollar commission."

"We're wholesalers, John." Cook smiled gently. "We would buy the time from you."

John fessed up. "Sorry, Harry, I'm new to this game."

"No problem. We all have to start somewhere. Let me tell you, by the way, that we have a triple-A credit rating, so you *will* get your money. Although I'm sure you'll be doing your due diligence on us, anyway."

If this was going somewhere, and it was looking as if it might, John would certainly be doing his due diligence. Harry Cook's next question took him completely by surprise.

"Could you take sixty people for four days from Tuesday of next week, and the same each week for the foreseeable future?"

John's brain was reeling. Talk about the right place at the right time. They were ready apart from bedding and towels. Sybille would have to take her finger out. "Yes, we could."

"Are you sure you wouldn't rather check and get back to me?"

"I don't need to check, Harry. We'll do it."

"Okay, then let me give you some background. We're working with a new feeder airline out of Fort Lauderdale and they'll be flying out sixty people every four days. Could you handle that much traffic?"

"We'll handle it," John said.

"Great, then we have a deal."

They shook hands across the table.

"Do you want to take a quick trip over to take a look?"

Cook shook his head. "I would do normally, John, but there isn't time. We've got flights booked and nowhere to put people. The property we had lined up just reneged on a deal. That's the trouble with the Bahamas; you can't trust people. It's nice to be dealing with an Englishman, because I know you won't let me down."

When John gave Sybille the news, instead of her reacting with even a modicum of enthusiasm, Sybille reacted with a laconic, "About time too."

John ignored her. "He'll mail you a cheque at the end of each month. Make sure you keep accurate records."

"I know what I need to do," Sybille said. "I don't need a lecture from you."

Chapter 27

When John next called the property, a female voice he did not recognise answered the phone. "Atlantic Beach Apartments. Gladys speaking. How may I help you?" John approved; she sounded professional, as if she had had prior experience. She was Bahamian, if her accent was anything to go by.

"This is John McLaren. You must be our new receptionist."

"Yes, sir. I am."

"Do you know who I am?"

"Yes, sir. Sybille's told me about you."

And I'll bet none of it flattering. "Is she there?"

There was a pause during which John heard muffled voices.

"I'm sorry, sir. She's off the property." Her tone had changed. It sounded like she was repeating verbatim something someone had said, and she was being careful to get it right.

John felt certain Sybille was standing right beside her, but he didn't want to put the new receptionist in an even more awkward position by being difficult with her. "Do you know when she'll be back?"

There was another pause. More muffled voices. "I'm sorry, sir. She didn't say."

"Gladys, would you happen to know if a Mr Harry Cook has been in touch with Sybille?"

"Yes, sir, he has."

"Have Sybille call me when she gets in, would you?"

"Certainly, sir."

"You don't have to call me sir, Gladys; John will do. We're on the same side."

John twiddled his thumbs at his desk for the rest of the morning. He went home for lunch, returned to his office and sat at his desk until five p.m., when he called the property again.

"Atlantic Beach Apartments. Gladys speaking. How may I help you?"

"It's John, Gladys. John McLaren."

"Oh, yes. Hello, Mr McLaren."

"Is Sybille back yet?"

"No, sir, I'm afraid she isn't."

"Has she been back since I called this morning?"

"Just a moment." Muffled voices. "Yes, she has been back, but she had to go out again."

"I see. Thank you, Gladys."

"You're welcome, sir. Have a nice evening."

John phoned the property at nine the next morning, and again at eleven. He phoned again at two, and five in the afternoon. Each time he got the same message. He sent a fax, but it was not answered.

Sybille had pulled up her drawbridge and her moat was the width of a fifty-minute flight.

John didn't call again until the morning of the day the airline business was due to start. There was a hubbub of voices in the background and Gladys sounded harassed. "Sir, may I call you back? I have an office full of people to attend to."

"Let me ask you a question, Gladys. Has Sybille left you to attend to those people on your own, or is she standing there beside you. And please don't lie to me this time."

There was a pause, and then the buzzing tone. The call had been disconnected. He knew Gladys would have valued her new job too much to hang up on him; it had to be Sybille. He slammed the phone down and drove home in a rage.

Liz said, "Get on a plane and go over and sort her out. She's never been able to get the better of you before, don't let her start now."

"And then what? Have her pull up the drawbridge again when I've left to come back? And if it came to the only other option; I don't know about you, but after all the crap we've had to put with from her, I sure as hell wouldn't want to go back there to live."

Over the next few days, John phoned the property morning and afternoon, always getting the same response: "I'm sorry, John, she's not on the property. I'll tell her you called." It was like talking to an answering machine.

"Why is she doing this to me, Liz?" John said, over his third large gin and tonic one evening. "I've plucked her from obscurity, she's got a fifty percent share in the property and I'm paying her a thousand dollars a week. What have I done to deserve this treatment?"

"I wouldn't take it personally, John. Do you remember what Rolly said about her planning to own the property and not giving up until she gets what she wants? I think that's exactly what she's doing. I think the only thing you can do is get over there and assert your authority."

"We've already covered that subject." He drained his glass and handed it to Liz. "Do you want to pour me another one?"

"John, you've had three large ones already."

"Who's counting?"

John lost interest in going to the office. What was the point? He was drinking heavily and he paced the apartment night after night, unable to sleep. At three-thirty one morning, Liz found him watching a black and white movie on TV. She sat down beside him and took his hand. "Darling, just get on a plane and go over there. I'll come with you if you like. I'm sure we could sort her out if we went together." He wouldn't listen. When she found him having a serious conversation with one of the alligators in the lake, she tried to get him to see a doctor. But he said he was fine, and to stop fussing.

John had no idea what turned him around, but one morning he leapt out of bed, waking Liz with a start, and demanding coffee. "I'll take it in the shower," he said. "I'm going to Freeport." When Liz took him his coffee, she found him scrubbing himself furiously, his face contorted with anger. He put on a suit and tie, had breakfast and went to the office.

There were no messages on his answering machine and no faxes. When he checked his desk diary, he discovered he had been out of action for ten weeks. He had no real recollection of events during that period, and thought he had probably had a nervous breakdown.

Before he went to Freeport he needed to know how much business had been transacted with Harry Cook. He picked up the phone.

"Hey there, buddy," Cook said. "Long time, no hear."

"Yes, sorry about that, Harry. I haven't been well. How's it going with the property?"

"It's going well. I'm impressed with Sybille. She's doing a great job."

"I knew she would. Harry, would you mind faxing me the details of the business to date. I just need to make sure our figures jibe with yours."

"No problem. How soon do you want the information?'

"Yesterday would be good."

"You bet. I'll get someone on it right away."

According to the fax John received within the hour, business worth $55,556.00 – to the property, that is – had been transacted. This had been settled by a cheque dated five weeks ago, the other dated a calendar month later. The fax indicated that the cheques had been couriered to the property, meaning there was virtually no chance of them being lost in the mail.

Next, John needed to know that the money had gone into the company account. He phoned the bank and asked to speak to Andy McTavish. He was told that Mr McTavish was not in the office today, and he was put through to his PA, Marion Barker, whom John had met.

"Good morning, John," she said. "Andy's not in at the moment. Can I help?"

"I'm sure you can, Marion," John said. "I need to check that a total of $55,556.00 has been deposited in the company account within the last four or five weeks. Two cheques were issued, so there should have been two deposits, about a month apart."

"I can tell you that without looking," Marion said. "Because Andy and I were discussing it only yesterday. We know there's been a lot of activity on the property and we've been expecting money to start flowing into the account. But there's been nothing."

John swore under his breath. "Will Andy be available tomorrow, Marion?"

"Yes, he should be here all day."

"Tell him to expect me in the morning. I'm not sure what time."

The only available flight to Freeport that day was early evening. John booked himself a seat, and then booked himself a room for the night. He then phoned DCI Johnson and told him he needed to see him, and why.

John wore a suit and travelled light: just his briefcase, which doubled as an overnight case. When he landed in Freeport he rented a car and drove straight to his hotel, where he phoned George Humphries. Humphries had asked him to keep him posted and he had proved to be an excellent listener, and a wise counsel as and when necessary. John had his best night's sleep in weeks, his body no doubt making up for lost time.

The next morning, John got to the police station around nine a.m., and he spent almost an hour with DCI Johnson. Marion Barker had faxed John the last two months bank statements, and he handed photocopies of these to the detective. He also handed him a copy of Harry Cook's fax so the detective would have documentary evidence that the two payments had been made.

Johnson studied the documents carefully, and then he asked, "Have you checked with the courier?"

"Yes, I have. Federal Express confirmed they were delivered the next day, in each case."

"And the signature?"

"My charming partner, Ms Sybille Johanssen."

Johnson nodded slowly. "Then we seem to have a prima facie case of misrepresentation of corporate funds. What are your plans for the rest of the day, Mr McLaren?"

"Please, call me John."

"Richard," the detective said.

John smiled briefly and nodded. "Well, from here, Richard, I'm going to the bank. Then I was planning to go to the property."

"Does Sybille know you're coming?"

"Not from me, she doesn't. I suppose there's a slim chance someone she knows has seen me since I arrived, although I've tried to make myself as inconspicuous as possible."

"Best not to let her know you've involved the police. No point giving her the chance to plan a strategy."

At the bank, Andy McTavish sighed. "I'm afraid the missing money is not all, John. Since you spoke to Marion yesterday, we've been doing some checking. Here, you'd better take a look at this." He handed John a photocopy of a completed application form for a bank account in the name of Atlantic Beach Apartments with a bank the name of which had been Tippexed out.

John read the first couple of paragraphs of the document and looked up in astonishment. "But she can't do this. She can't open an account without board approval, and I certainly didn't authorise this."

"You'd better read on, John. She appointed another director."

"She did *what*? She can't do *that*! That's illegal, for Christ's sake."

"Tell me about it," the banker said. "I'm informed that she arrived at the bank in question with a man by the name of Enrico Rodrigues, a lawyer known to most of us as a shyster, and a Bahamian woman. They held a board meeting in the manager's office and appointed the woman a director of the company."

John sighed. "Rolly was right. She'll stop at nothing to get what she wants."

"Sorry?"

"Nothing, I was just thinking aloud. But wouldn't the bank manager have smelled a rat, Sybille arriving mob-handed and holding a board meeting in his office? Especially if he knew the lawyer to be a shyster."

"I certainly would, I would have shown her the door. But things sometimes happen here in the Bahamas that shouldn't happen."

"Who was the woman?" John asked.

"Her name's on the document."

John looked further down the document. The name was Gladys Richards. The only Gladys he knew was the new receptionist. "Now I'll believe anything," he said.

"Do you know the woman, John?"

"I've never actually met her, but I'm pretty sure she's our new receptionist."

"Smart thinking on Sybille's part," the banker said. "With good jobs hard to find, she'll probably do whatever Sybille tells her."

"Jesus, what a bloody nightmare."

"I'm afraid there's more." McTavish handed John a photocopy of another bank document. The name of this bank had been obliterated, too. "She also applied for a mortgage on the property."

"She did *what*! For how much, for God's sake?"

"A hundred and fifty thousand dollars."

"You're kidding!"

"She apparently said that, in exchange for the fifty-five thousand dollars she was depositing, she wanted a mortgage."

"Ah, so now we come to the two cheques. Andy, *please* tell me she didn't get the mortgage money."

"I'm happy to report that she didn't."

"Thank God for that!"

"But if you hadn't spoken to Marion yesterday she would have. It was that close. It had been approved."

"This is too much." John shook his head in disbelief.

"Well, she won't be doing anything like this again, I promise you that. She has cooked her goose well and truly. She'll be lucky if she can find a bank that will touch her after this. The word is out."

"What about the two cheques, Andy?"

"I don't know, John. There's a limit to what I can find out; Bahamian banking secrecy laws being what they are. I think

145

the best thing you can do is contact whoever issued the cheques and, if the cheques have not cleared their account, ask them to cancel them and wire the money into the company account. And you might want to ask them to adopt this procedure from now on."

"Good thinking," John said. "And there's no time like the present. Can I use your phone?"

On the property, a trestle table had been set up in the gardens and an attractive black woman was dispensing cocktails to a group of twenty to thirty people. Sybille was mingling. She looked happy and relaxed, the consummate hostess. When she saw John, her smile vanished. "Not now," she mouthed.

"Yes, now," he mouthed, nodding. He pointed to the office.

Sybille had made some changes in the office, changes of which he approved. She had put the desk in what had previously been the dining area and she had arranged the furniture in the living room in such a way as to provide a spacious and comfortable sitting area for people waiting to be checked in.

On the walls were framed photographs of Sybille on and around dive boats, and there was another photograph, one which annoyed him, of Sybille posing by his boat with the name SYBILLE ONE standing out like a beacon. She had yet to make the first payment on the boat.

Sybille had moved the effigies. They were now standing on a worktop in the kitchen. He could see from where he stood that there were three pins in his effigy, and no doubt he would be getting more when Sybille learned what he had been up to.

Sybille walked in and closed the door. She flopped on to the new sofa. "So, you finally decided to put in an appearance."

John remained standing. "You've been a busy girl," he said.

Sybille obviously thought he was referring to how she had rearranged the office. "Yes, it does look good," she said, looking round the room and admiring her handiwork. "That's not what I was referring to. You think you're clever, don't you, Sybille?"

"I suppose I do have my moments."

"Have you heard the expression what goes around come around?"

"Of course I have, but that doesn't apply to me because I'm not superstitious. Can I make you a coffee, before you leave? For old time's sake."

Chapter 28

When John got back to Orlando and stepped through the door of their rented apartment Liz planted a kiss on his lips and asked him how he had got on with US Immigration.

John held up his hand with his thumb and forefinger a half inch apart. "I came this close to them not letting me in."

"You poor love," Liz said. "It must have been very stressful."

"It was, and a large gin and tonic would not go amiss."

He hung his jacket over a chair and walked out on to the deck. The light was fading and, in the gloom, he saw one of the alligators stalking a duck, its snout and its eyes the only parts of its anatomy visible to the naked eye. He sat down to watch the drama unfold.

The duck realised the danger when a mouth the size of a small cave opened behind it. There was an almighty squawk and the poor creature flapped its wings and tried desperately to take off. But it was too late; the mouth clamped shut and the alligator sank beneath the surface, leaving a flurry of feathers and a swirl of water to mark the spot where the bird began its journey to its final resting place on the great duck pond in the sky.

For a moment, John imagined it was Sybille clamped in the jaws of the reptile. That would solve some problems.

Liz walked out with three fingers of gin and tonic in a tumbler, the ice clinking merrily against the glass, and a glass of white wine for herself.

"Glad to be home?" she said, handing him his drink.

"Very. It's been quite a day." He acquainted her with the day's events. "She's going to be apoplectic when she finds out what I've done."

The message on his answering machine at the office two days later was succinct and to the point. "Where the fuck are you? Call me."

He picked up the phone.

"Atlantic Beach Apartments. Gladys speaking. How may I help you?"

"Gladys, it's John."

"Oh, hello, John. I'm sorry I didn't get the chance to talk to you when you were on the property the other day. I was a bit tied up at the time."

"So I noticed. Are you enjoying your job?"

"Very much. Did you want to speak to Sybille?"

"Yes, please."

"One second, John."

There was a pause, and then Sybille's dulcet tones. "Where the fuck have you been?"

He grinned. "You say the nicest things, Sybille."

"You've fucked up big time, this time."

"Have I?"

"Cut the crap, John. You know what I'm talking about."

"Let's for a moment assume that I don't have a clue what you're talking about, so why don't you enlighten me?"

"Where do you want me to start?"

"The beginning is often a good place to start?"

"Very well, I'll start with the mortgage. Why did you put a stop to it?"

"I didn't."

"Well someone did."

"I'm sorry to disappoint you, Sybille, but it wasn't me."

"If it wasn't you, who was it?"

"If I told you that I'd have to kill you."

"Be serious, John. This is not funny."

For you it might not be, but some of us are having a hilarious time. "Sorry, I'll try to be serious. Next?"

"The cheques."

"What about them?"

"You've had them cancelled."

"What did you expect when you were trying to open another account with them?"

"How did you find out?"

"A little bird told me."

"You can be maddening at times, John."

"So I've been told. Was there something else, Sybille?"

"Yes, there was. I've had another visit from the police."

"My, we are getting popular. That's twice in ... how long has it been?"

"Behave! Why did you involve them?"

"What would you have done if you'd found yourself in the position I found myself in?"

"You've gone too far this time, John. I want you out of my life."

John punched the air and emitted a big fat silent YES! "I'm listening."

"I'm going to buy you out."

"Fine, but that begs the question: with what will you buy me out?"

"With the money from the airline business."

"Nice try, Sybille, but that isn't your money."

"Then I'll bring in money from outside."

"If it's drugs money you're talking about, you can forget it."

"What does it matter where the money comes from?"

"It matters to me."

"Then you buy me out."

"Sybille," John said cautiously, "that may be possible, but it's going to mean some considerable thought from my side. I've sunk most of my capital into the property."

"Well don't take too long. Otherwise I'll walk out of here and you and that wife of yours can come back and run this place yourselves."

Chapter 29

In determining what to offer Sybille for her share in the property, John wanted to be scrupulously fair.

Included in his calculations as to what he had spent, were: the renovations, including the air-conditioning, furniture, carpets, fixtures and fittings, towels, bedding, etc.; the monthly payments made to Enrico Rodrigues and the wages to Sybille, the gardener, Gladys and the two chambermaids, and lawyer's fees. And, since he knew with a high degree of certainty that Sybille would never pay him for his boat, he added in what the boat had cost him.

He called Nicholas Truckle to ask him how long he thought it would take to get the injunction lifted.

"Better give me a year," the lawyer said. "To be on the safe side."

John then calculated a year of profit based on the present level of occupancy. They had all their eggs in one basket, which was not ideal, but he had nothing else to go on. He then added what he thought the sale of forty-two apartments would yield. From the resultant total, he deducted his costs. He then divided the net result by two, to take into account that there were two parties to consider – Liz and himself, and Sybille.

Then, knowing from a lifetime of business experience that nothing ever works out the way you want it to, he reduced this figure by a quarter.

He then spent two days in the peace and quiet of his office wording a letter to Sybille. He explained in detail on what he was basing his offer and, after producing draft after draft, he finally achieved the wording he was looking for. He asked Liz to cast her eyes over the letter, and then he phoned the courier company.

Thirty-six hours later, he received a faxed reply from Sybille. *I'm sorry, John, but this doesn't work for me. Please call me.*

Rarely had Sybille used such a moderate tone, so at least he was making progress. He picked up the phone.

"Atlantic Beach Apartments. Gladys speaking. How may I help you?"

"Gladys, it's John. Is Sybille there?"

"She's not on the property at the moment, John, but she left word that, if you called, she would return your call when she got back."

Sybille phoned a couple of hours later. "I can see where you're coming from with your offer, John," she said, "but it doesn't work for me."

"It's not cast in stone, Sybille. If you'd like to tell me why it doesn't work for you, perhaps I can do something about it."

There was a pause. "Can I make a suggestion?"

"Of course you can."

"Well, as I see it, there's no point in us to-ing and fro-ing at a distance, because it could go on for weeks. I think that if we sit down across my desk, and look into each other's eyes as we talk, we can thrash out something that works for both of us."

Sybille was making perfect sense, but John had US Immigration to think about, and he told her so. "Perhaps you could come to Orlando," he said.

"I would if I could, John, but with so many people to take care of, I couldn't get away. Couldn't you tell the immigration people you won't have to make the trip again? I've lied to them loads of times."

John knew it would be far from the last trip he would have to make if he bought Sybille out, and he certainly wasn't going to start lying to US Immigration – that was a rock he would probably perish on, but he also knew that, if he was going to get her out of his hair once and for all, he had no choice. "All right, Sybille," he said. "I'll come there."

Chapter 30

"Don't worry, I'm not anticipating any problems."

"I wish you hadn't said that," Liz said. "You're tempting providence."

"Hey, come on," John said cheerfully. "I'll be fine."

It was 0800 hours and John was sitting in his car with the engine running and the window down. His flight was scheduled to leave Orlando International at 1000 hours. Liz was standing by the car. This was a business trip and he was wearing a suit, which always put him in the mood for business. His document case, containing his passport, a photocopy of his offer to Sybille, a legal pad and a spare ballpoint pen, lay on the seat beside him.

"Do be careful, John. You know what she's like."

"I will." John shifted the automatic into drive mode, keeping his foot on the brake.

Liz pecked him on the cheek. "I love you."

"I love you too. I should be home around ten, assuming the flight's on time. And Immigration let me in." He grinned.

"It's not Immigration I'm worried about. Have a safe trip."

Sybille was waiting for him in the arrivals hall at Freeport airport and, in a man's long-sleeved shirt, frayed jeans and open-toed sandals, she was dressed more for the beach than for business.

"What's this?" he said, annoyed. "I come dressed for business, and you come dressed for the beach."

"Change of plan," Sybille said, smiling sweetly. "You've never been out on your boat, have you, John?"

"No, but I'm hardly dressed for boating. And you said you couldn't …"

"I just thought that, since it's such a beautiful day, we should get out on the water. I thought we'd go to a little island I know. I've made sandwiches and coffee and we can talk business when we get there. You do like tuna and mayonnaise, don't you?"

"Yes, I do, but ..."

"What time's your flight home."

"Eight-thirty. I need to be here by seven-thirty. But ..."

"That's fine, I'll have you back in plenty of time for that. I do like your suit, by the way. I don't think I've seen that suit before. How's Liz? Is she well?"

John had seen her in this mood before and he knew he wasn't going to get any sense out of her so, with a sigh of resignation, he trooped along behind her to her 4x4.

The boat was in a smallish off-the-beaten-track marine equipped with a brick-built office building and a chandlery. There was no shortage of boats. There were only a handful of cars in the car park and Sybille was able to park near the boat.

John noticed that Sybille had had radar fitted; the antennae was on the tee-top, together with four powerful-looking spotlights. And she had also had the transom modified and a second engine fitted. All of which begged the question: where had she got the money?

In the back of Sybille's vehicle were two scuba tanks. "Would you mind putting those on the boat, John?" she said. "They're full, and they're quite heavy."

"Are you planning to dive today?"

"I thought I might, after I've got you back to the airport."

John tucked his document case under his arm. The tanks were heavy, but not so heavy he couldn't pick up one in each hand. He carried them to the boat, hefted them over the side and laid them on the deck. He put his document case on one of the seats and then walked back to the vehicle. "Anything else, Sybille?"

"Just those." Sybille pointed to a cooler and thermos flask. "I'll manage the rest." She picked up a pair of fins, facemask and snorkel. Then she picked up a baseball bat.

"What's the baseball bat for? Are you planning to hit me over the head with it?"

"Don't tempt me," Sybille said. "I use it for protection. I always carry it when I'm out on the water. A girl can't be too careful."

John had heard horrific stories of women getting caught alone on Bahamian waters and he didn't blame Sybille for carrying some form of protection. He put the cooler on the deck, and stood the flask upright on one of the seats.

Sybille tossed her fins, snorkel and face mask on a seat, and then she lifted an adjoining seat and dropped the baseball bat into the storage space beneath it. "No point in advertising that I'm carrying it," she said. "Would you untie the stern line, John? I'll take the bow."

John untied the stern line and stepped aboard.

Sybille untied the bow lie, pushed the boat with her foot to get it moving away from the dock, and then hopped aboard. She took up station at the centre console and took the ignition key, which was attached to a golf-ball sized piece of cork, from her pocket and put it in the ignition. She patted the leaning post beside her.

John got the message and parked himself beside her.

"All set?" she said.

"All set."

Sybille turned the ignition key and the engines burbled into life, belching out black smoke and an unpleasant oily smell. Since she didn't seem concerned by this, John ignored it. She put the boat in gear, eased the throttle forward and spun the wheel, easing the boat away from the dock.

A man with epaulets on the shoulders of his jersey stepped out of the office building. "Don't forget there's a tropical storm due, Sybille," he said. "And it's going to be a big one, so don't be out too long."

"We won't, Horace," Sybille said. "We're not going far."

John wasn't a good sailor at the best of times and this news filled him with dread. "Are you sure about this, Sybille?" he asked nervously. "Shouldn't we just go and talk in the office?"

"Relax," Sybille said. "You'll be tucked up in your bed in Orlando before the storm gets anywhere near here. It's over Bermuda right now. It must be a thousand miles away."

John looked up at the sky, and slowly turned around. There was unbroken blue sky wherever he looked. "Well, if you're sure," he said.

Sybille drove carefully between two rows of parked boats. "By the way," she said, "I've never told you how well I thought you did in getting us the airline business. It's great that we got so much business, so quickly. I couldn't have done it."

Since this was the first time Sybille had ever paid him a compliment, John was momentarily nonplussed. Finally, he said, "Let's put it down to me being in the right place at the right time."

Sybille was having none of it. "Absolutely not. Credit where credit's due. If you hadn't done what you did, we wouldn't have got the business. So, well done you."

"Well, thank you, Sybille. It's kind of you to say so." John couldn't help thinking what a difference if would have made if Sybille had been as nice as this from the outset.

Access to the marina for boats was by a canal on the bank of which was a sign advising of a ten mile-per-hour speed limit. A few yards further along was another sign, this one advising boat owners they were responsible for any damage their bow wave caused.

After about a mile the canal opened into a deep-water channel which John recognised as being the channel which ran alongside the development in which he and Liz had lived. As they motored past the development John looked to his left to see if he could see anyone he knew, and he saw Rolly Schaerer was standing by the swimming pool chatting with a couple of men in suits. He was pointing to the newest of the three buildings and talking earnestly, no doubt trying to talk the men into a multi-million dollar deal. John thought to call out to him but, not wanting to distract his friend, he thought better of it.

They motored on past the rocks where he and Liz and fished and, remembering some of the amusing times they had had, he smiled.

"Bring back memories?" Sybille said.

"Yes, and happy ones. Liz and I used to fish from here."

"You're a lucky man, John."

"Am I? Why am I lucky?"

"Because you can afford to live in beautiful apartments on beautiful beaches."

"Luck has very little to with it, Sybille. I've worked for everything I have. Nothing has been handed to me on a plate."

When they were clear of the headland, Sybille rammed the throttle control forward and yelled, "Hang on!" The engines howled and launched the boat on to the plane.

John held on for dear life as the boat bucked and bounced through the waves. Every time the boat hit a wave heavy spray cascaded over the bow and, were he not protected by the screen, he would have been drenched. The wind whistled round the screen, the hull banged on the waves, and the engines howled. It was a mad cacophony of sound. John laughed and laughed, and Sybille laughed with him. He suspected she was showing off, but he was having such a good time that he couldn't have cared less.

Sybille was leaning against the post with her shoes off and her ankles crossed. She looked at him and grinned. "It doesn't get much better than this," she yelled.

"No it doesn't," he yelled. His words caught in his throat as the boat hit a wave. He pointed to the illuminated screen of the satellite navigation device. "Do you find that useful?" he yelled.

"I couldn't manage without it," Sybille yelled. "It takes me wherever I want to go."

"How do you enter coordinates?"

Sybille showed him.

"Have you put the coordinates in for your island?" he yelled.

"Yes, I have. Although I'd be able to find my way there without them, now."

They had been travelling for about five minutes when Sybille brought the boat off the plane. She brought it to a standstill and knocked it out of gear. It rocked gently on the swell.

John's ears were ringing.

"We're over the reef," Sybille said. "Where we fished that evening with Liz, and Rolly."

John peered at the shoreline. He could just make out the roof of the shed where the dolphins from Dive With The Dolphins were penned. "So we are," he said.

Sybille stepped to the side of the boat and beckoned him. "Take a look."

John stepped to the side of the boat and looked down. With the sun shining through the water, the seabed looked almost close enough to touch, despite the water being forty to fifty feet deep. The last time they were here there had been nothing but inky blackness. The reef was ablaze with colour and the water teemed with fish.

"I was going to bring Liz here at some point," Sybille said, steadying herself as a wave rocked the boat. "She learns quickly, that wife of yours."

"I know she does. Speaking of Rolly, Sybille, what happened between the two of you? Tell me to mind my own business if you like."

"I'd rather not talk about it, if you don't mind, John. It's still quite raw. Shall we go on? We have some distance to go, yet."

"Okay."

"Would you like to drive?"

Would I? Yes, please. John grinned. "I thought you'd never ask." He stepped to the centre console and took his position at the wheel.

Sybille settled herself beside him. "Right," she said briskly, "there are two things to think about: speed, and direction. You know how to control the speed …" she tapped the throttle control … "and, if you follow the instructions the sat nav gives you, you'll get us there. Any questions?"

"Nope."

"Then I'm going to take a nap. Wake me when we get there." She made her way to the front of the boat and lay down on the cushioned storage lockers.

John started the engines and put the boat in gear. He eased the throttle lever forward. The boat moved forward and started to wallow alarmingly. He pushed the throttle control further forward. The boat picked up speed and the wallowing decreased. Finally, he did what Sybille had done, he shoved the throttle control forward as far as it would go. The boat launched itself on to the plane. He trimmed the speed and settled down to enjoy himself.

Sybille lay facing him. In sleep, she looked like butter wouldn't melt in her mouth. But, as Andy McTavish had remarked, people who indulge in drug running look just like the rest of us.

John was beginning to wonder if they would ever get to their destination, when he saw a line of pine trees dead ahead. They looked to be sprouting from the ocean. "Is this the place, Sybille?" he called, waking her.

Sybille sat up and peered over the bow. "Yes, this is it." She stretched and yawned and then got to her feet. "I'll take it from here," she said.

John stepped aside to let her take the wheel.

"Did you enjoy driving?" she said.

"Very much."

"I thought you would."

Sybille's island looked to be little more than a sand bar with trees. It was about a hundred yards long, by fifty yards wide. It was possible to see the water on the other side of the island, through the trees. Her idea of her island being *not far* had taken an hour and a half of hard driving to reach.

Sybille slowed the boat down and drove to within about thirty yards off the beach, and then cut the engines and tossed out the anchor.

The sudden silence was deafening. There was not even the cawing of a seagull to be heard. The only sounds to be heard were the crackling of the engines, as they cooled, and the lapping of the water on the hull of the boat.

"Are you ready for a sandwich?"

"I certainly am, I'm hungry. And then perhaps we can get down to talking business."

"No problem." Sybille opened the cooler and withdrew a sandwich wrapped in cling-film. She handed it to him. Then she unscrewed the cup on the thermos flask, filled it with coffee and handed that to him. "I'm sorry, John, I've forgotten the sugar. I hope you don't mind."

John hated the taste of coffee without sugar, but he waved her apology away. She was being so nice to him that he wouldn't have complained if the coffee had been stone cold.

Sybille took a polystyrene cup from the cooler and poured herself some coffee. She then took a couple of pills from a wrap of soft tissue in her pocket, popped them in her mouth, and washed them down.

"Are you not eating?" John said, unwrapping his sandwich.

Sybille shook her head. "I don't eat at lunchtime. But you enjoy your sandwich, John. And there's no need to hurry; we have all the time in the world."

Chapter 31

John never knew what hit him. The baseball bat caught him behind the left ear. He dropped like a stone.

Sybille stood over him, her chest heaving. She dropped the baseball bat and knelt beside him. There was no blood. She hated the sight of blood, despite having been a nurse in Canada. She felt his pulse. It was weak and thready. She was relieved he was still alive. If his body was ever found, it was important to her story that he was found to have died from drowning.

She took off her shirt and jeans to reveal a one-piece bathing costume. The track marks on her arm itched, and she scratched them, flinching when she inadvertently picked off a scab.

John was lying face down. She grabbed him under the arms and, heaving for all she was worth, got him to the side of the boat. Another heave and he was hanging over the side. Another heave and his head and torso were in the water, and one final heave and he was in the water. He sank five or six feet below the surface and then slowly resurfaced, inexplicably turning over on to his back.

His effigy, which now had five pins in it, was in a compartment in the centre console, and Sybille took it out and tossed it over the side. It was so light it barely made a splash. It landed by John's shoulder, and Sybille found John floating side-by-side with his effigy somehow rather satisfying. A sort of poetic justice for all the things he had messed up for her.

She then put on her scuba gear and sat on the edge of the boat and fell in, backwards. Treading water she dipped her facemask in the water, spat on the inside of the glass, to prevent the glass misting up, and then put on the mask.

She grabbed John round the waist and dragged him down to the seabed some fifteen feet below. When she was satisfied he was dead, she left him there and swam back to the surface to collect his effigy.

Sybille had her own set of rules when it came to where she buried effigies: she buried them where she knew she would be able to find them again, in case, at some point in the future, she had a change of heart. She looked for a reference point on the island and found it in the form of two pine saplings standing about twenty feet apart. She manoeuvred herself into a position midway between the saplings, effectively making herself the apex of a triangle with them, then upended herself and swam as near vertically as she could down to the seabed.

Another of Sybille's idiosyncrasies was that she buried effigies standing up. She had no recollection of why she did this; it had just sort of ... evolved. Since the effigy was about eight inches high, and there needed to be at least two inches of sand over its head, it was going to need a hole at least ten inches deep. And, since the effigy was made of polystyrene and would have floated to the surface if she had let go of it, she had to dig the hole with one hand.

When, finally, she judged the hole deep enough, she shoved the effigy into it, feet first, and wiggled it around to make sure it was firmly embedded in the sand. She then swam to the surfaced, took one more look at the two saplings, and then swam to the boat.

She hauled herself aboard and, shading her eyes against the sun, quickly scanned the area. There were no boats in the area, ergo no witnesses. There were some clouds some distance to the south, which she had not noticed before, but there was otherwise nothing but blue sky and green water.

She took off her bathing costume and struggled into her shirt and jeans, cursing herself for her stupidity in forgetting to bring a towel to dry herself with. She sat for a moment to get her breath, and then dug a small twist of soft tissue from a pocket in her jeans, and took out two of six small white pills.

She tossed them in her mouth and washed them down with the now-cold remnants of the coffee in the Styrofoam cup she had been using.

She knew the coordinates for Freeport off by heart because she came here whenever she could; it gave her time alone, and she set them into the satellite navigation device. She then hauled in the anchor, started the engines and howled away. Ten minutes later, she tossed the baseball bat over the side. She defied anyone to find a baseball bat in the vastness of the Atlantic Ocean.

She deliberately drove close to flat out, her rationale for this being that, if she arrived back at the marina with her engines crackling with heat, it would lend credence to her story that there had been a boating accident and that she had driven back flat out so Air and Sea Rescue could send out a search party as soon as possible. As to why she had not reported the accident on her ship-to-shore radio when it happened, and she knew the police would ask her this, she would tell them that there was a fault with the device and that she had reported this to the boat dealer, and that he had told her to take the boat in and he would fix it, and that she had never got around to doing it, because she had never actually needed the device. All of which was true.

Sybille was so preoccupied with rehearsing the story she had concocted for the police that she failed to notice that the ocean had become a flat calm, and it was only when a blast of cold air buffeted her from behind that she realised something was amiss. She turned and was horrified to see a mass of angry black cloud.

Within minutes, the wind was howling and huge waves were building. The sky blackened and it began to rain. The temperature plummeted. The tee-top afforded scant protection, as the wind whipped the rain in from the sides. She switched on the four spotlights, but this just illuminated the mountainous seas and the driving rain. The boat rose on the waves, and fell into the troughs on the other side, and Sybille was violently sick. The waves were running mostly from behind, but Sybille had the presence of mind to also watch for waves coming from the sides and, when she saw one coming, she spun the wheel furiously so she met the wave head on.

She was soaking wet and shivering with cold and she popped two more pills in her mouth. She had nothing to swallow them with and almost choked as she tried to swallow them dry. She gritted her teeth and ploughed on.

After what seemed an eternity, she became aware of lights dead ahead. She realised, in the nick of time, that they were the lights from the hotel at the entrance to the channel and, by dramatically reducing her speed and furiously spinning the wheel, she narrowly avoided running on to the rocks.

Sybille had worked out how to disable the satellite navigation device and, as she motored slowly up the channel and the apartment buildings provided momentary protection from the wind, she disabled it.

When she got to her marina, boats were pitching and tossing and straining at their lines, like savage dogs anxious to be let off their leashes. Some had broken free of their moorings and were plunging around like wild mustangs.

As she approached her dock, a huge gust of wind hit her from behind. It was like being hit by a truck. The boat surged forward, ramming the dock. There was the sound of splintering wood and shattering fibreglass and Sybille slammed the boat into reverse. It lurched backwards, pitching her forwards and banging her head on the windscreen, momentarily dazing her. She shook her head, to clear it, and then looked for someone to whom she could report a boating accident. Hardly surprisingly, the marina was deserted. There were no lights in the office building, or in the chandlery. They had shut up shop and gone home.

At her third attempt, Sybille docked the boat successfully. She shut down the engines and flung out the lines, leaping on to the dock before the wind had a chance to blow the boat away. She had to blow on her freezing fingers to get enough feeling in them to tie the knots.

With the boat secured, Sybille braved the gale and the driving rain to inspect it for damage. There was a hole in the bow, but it was a couple of feet above the water line so there was no immediate danger of the boat taking on water and sinking.

It took two trips to get her scuba gear into her 4x4, and she then ran back to the bucking boat and jumped aboard again to make sure she had not missed anything incriminating, which the police might find.

John's document case lay on the deck and Sybille picked it up. It was limp and sodden, the beautiful red leather now ruined. Out of curiosity, she took a peek inside and got a glimpse of a legal pad and a passport. She closed it up again and dropped it where it had lain before.

Then, satisfied there was no evidence to contradict the story she had dreamed up, she jumped off the boat and ran to her vehicle. She started the engine and turned the heater up. She was soaked to the skin and the cold air issuing from the vents chilled her to the marrow.

She switched on the light above her rear-view mirror and took a quick look at herself. She hardly recognised the woman looking back at her. Her eyes were bloodshot with dark circles under, and the rest of her emaciated face was the colour of chalk. She knew she had been losing weight, and she knew why: the drugs she took were suppressing her appetite; almost to the point she had to force herself to eat.

She turned on the vehicle's headlights, illuminating the rain and leaves and twigs and other debris being hurled around. She turned on her windscreen wipers, cranking them up to full to try to cope with the volume of water cascading down her windscreen, put the vehicle in gear, let off the handbrake and drove away.

Chapter 32

Sybille desperately needed a fix and, since there were no witnesses as to when she had arrived back at the marina, instead of driving straight to the police station she drove to the property. She kept her drugs paraphernalia in a compartment behind her bathroom cabinet.

When she got to the property, she parked in the space marked *Manager* and leapt out of the vehicle. She tucked her head down and ran through the pelting rain. As she ran through the gardens, she noticed to her dismay that three trees were down, including her favourite queen palm. The good news was that the staff had had the good sense to throw the garden furniture into the pool. Hotel staff did this when there was a storm brewing; it ensured that outdoor furniture was not picked up by the wind and tossed through a window. She ran up the concrete steps and along the walkway to her apartment.

There were lights on in most of the apartments. The property was proving popular and the airline was ramping up the business.

As she entered her apartment, the wind caught the door and slammed it against the living room wall. She had to lean against the door to shut it. She switched on the living room lights and headed for the bathroom.

She was exhausted and she decided to take a quick nap. Since, if she arrived at the police station in dry clothes she couldn't claim to have come straight from the boat, she left her wet clothes on. Before she closed her eyes, she checked her watch. It was 6:05 p.m.

She had a dream in which John's bloated body floated to the surface and opened its eyes and leered at her, and she awoke with a start. She looked at her watch. It was 7:35 p.m. "Oh, shit!" She rolled off the bed, put on her wet shoes and headed for the door.

Because her clothes had partially dried while she had slept, she forced herself to walk through the teeming rain to her vehicle, rather than run. She adopted the same procedure when she got to the police station, as a result of which, when she walked into the building, her hair was plastered to her face and water was running freely off the end of her nose. Law enforcement officers stopped and stared as she approached the front desk.

The desk sergeant was completing a form with his head down and at first he didn't hear her.

She coughed to get his attention.

He looked up. "Oh, my," he said. "What have we here?"

"There's been a boating accident," Sybille said hoarsely. "My partner's missing and I think he's been drowned." Her eyes filled up.

"Right," the desk sergeant said briskly, "before we do anything else, let's see if I can find you a towel." He went away and came back with a threadbare, but clean, towel he had found in the men's washroom.

Sybille accepted it gratefully.

"Right, now let's get you sat down and then I'll see if I can organise some tea. My old mum used to say there was nothing like hot tea for someone in shock." He led Sybille into an interview room with a table on which obscene suggestions had been carved, and four chairs. The room reeked of stale cigarette smoke and there were cigarette burns along the edges of the table. There was a small, barred, window up near the ceiling in one of the walls.

The desk sergeant pulled out a chair for her. "Sit yourself here," he said. "I'll be back in a jiffy."

While he was away, Sybille dried her hair with the towel and ran through her story.

The desk sergeant came back with a chipped mug of tea, which he put on the table in front of her. "There, that should do the trick." He sat down across the table from her. "Now," he said in a kindly tone of voice, "what's this about a boating accident?"

Sybille took a sip of tea and put the mug down. The words tumbled out. "We were on the boat ... I went for a dive while he took a nap ... when I got back, he wasn't there. I searched and searched, but ... it was awful. I'll never forgive myself." Tears poured down her cheeks. It was a performance worthy of an Oscar.

"There now, don't distress yourself. When did this happen?"

"I didn't notice the time. Probably about one-thirty."

"One-thirty when? This afternoon?"

"Yes."

The desk sergeant looked at the clock on the wall, and frowned. "But that's six hours ago. Why are you only reporting this now?"

The words tumbled out again. "He'd come over to talk about buying me out ... and we went a long way out, because he'd never been out on the boat ... and when I couldn't find him ... and then I got caught in the storm." The tears rolled down her cheeks again.

The desk sergeant shoved back his chair and got to his feet. "We need to get Air and Sea Rescue in on this. He might still be alive."

Sybille sipped her tea. She heard the desk sergeant's voice from down the corridor. "George, it's Bob Heskin. There's been a boating accident. Can you get over here? Okay, see you then."

He came back with a pad and pencil.

Sybille's hands were shaking again. She had perfected the shaky hands ploy over the years, and the tears. She was particularly good with the tears.

"Right, let's get some details. Let's start with your name."

"Sybille Johanssen."

The lead in his pencil snapped. "Don't go away," he said. He got to his feet, tossed his pencil on the table, and marched down the corridor to the offices of CID.

DCI Richard Johnson was at his desk studying a report. He looked up when the desk sergeant entered. "Storm seems to be getting worse," he said. "Phone lines are down now. What can I do for you, Bob?"

"If I told you Sybille Johanssen was sitting in our interview room, what would you say?"

"I would say that was a remarkable coincidence," Johnson said, briefly waving the report he was reading. "This is the latest report on her. Tell me, Bob, did she come in of her own accord, or was she dragged in kicking and screaming?"

Under normal circumstances the desk sergeant would have found this amusing. Under the present circumstances he did not. "She came in to report a boating accident. She thinks her business partner's been drowned. George Humphries is on his way."

Johnson felt the blood drain from his face. "Are we talking about John McLaren?"

"I didn't get around to asking his name. When I realised who she was, I thought you might want to be involved."

"You thought right. Lead the way." Johnson followed the desk sergeant into the interview room and got right to the point. "What's this about a boating accident?"

"It's John," Sybille said, her bottom lip quivered and her eyes filled up. "It's just awful. I think he might be ..." She left the sentence unfinished.

"When did this happen?"

"Early this afternoon."

"Have you taken leave of your senses, going out on the water when a category five storm was imminent?"

"I thought we'd be back in time." The tears rolled down her cheeks.

Johnson took a seat at the far end of the table. He wanted to sit as far from Sybille as he could, so he could watch her body language as she answered his questions. "So tell me what happened."

"I need to get back to the desk," the desk sergeant said.

"All right, Bob. Go on, *Ms* Johanssen."

Sybille knew from her recent encounters with DCI Johnson that he was nobody's fool, and she could see from the way he was looking at her that she was going to have to be very careful about what she said. She took a deep breath. "John flew over this morning. He came to talk to me about buying me out. He said he'd like to go out on his boat. Did you know I was buying his boat?"

"Yes, he told me the last time I met him."

"Well, I told him it would be better if we talked on the property, but he insisted. I didn't want to upset him ..."

"No, of course you didn't."

"... So I took him to a small island I've found."

"Which was where?"

"About an hour and half's drive to the south."

"Why so far?"

"Because he wanted to drive. He said he might not get another chance."

"It sounds as if he might have got that right. And then what happened?"

"He said he was tired and wanted to take a nap. He said we could talk business afterwards. I decided to take a dive while he slept, and when I got back he wasn't there."

"How long were you away from the boat?"

"An hour, maybe. I'm not sure exactly. It could have been more."

"Go on."

"Well, I drove around looking for him for at least an hour, and then I drove back here as fast as I could. I don't know what else to tell you."

Johnson began to tap the table with his fingernail. Short sharp taps. He did this when something really annoyed him. "I have to say Ms. Johanssen, that knowing the history between you and Mr McLaren, I'm having difficulty believing this."

Sybille shrugged a see-if-I-care-if-you-believe-me shrug. "I'm only telling you what happened."

There was the sound of a sudden rush of air followed by a door slamming. Then a booming voice: "Bloody weather."

"In the interview room, George." It was the voice of the desk sergeant.

"Bloody wind blew my brolly inside out. I thought I was about to do a Mary Poppins and fly over the island."

When George Humphries saw Sybille, his faced changed. "What the hell are you doing here?"

"She reported the incident," Johnson said.

"Accident," Sybille said. "It was a boating accident."

"Until proved otherwise, I prefer to call it an incident."

Humphries leaned his ruined umbrella against the wall and took off his oilskin coat and hung it on a hook on the back of the incident room door. "So, what is this accident, or incident, or whatever you're going to call it?"

"John McLaren's gone missing at sea," Johnson said.

Humphries frowned. "What do you mean by missing?"

"Why don't you tell Mr Humphries what you've just told me," Johnson said. It was an instruction, not a question.

An irritated look crossed Sybille's face. "How many times do I have to repeat it?"

"As many times as I tell you to, or until you convince me you're telling the truth," Johnson said.

"You're treating me like a criminal, and all I did was come to report an accident."

"When you're ready," Johnson said.

Sybille glared at him and then went through her spiel again.

Humphries let her get to the point where she had got back to the boat after her dive, and found John missing, and then he said, "The boat has ship-to-shore radio, so why didn't you call it in?"

"I would have, but I couldn't," Sybille said. "The radio has a fault. It isn't working."

"Why isn't it working?" Humphries said. "It's a new boat."

"I reported the fault to the dealer and he told me to bring the boat in, but I never got around to it."

"What's the name of the dealer?" Johnson asked.

"Alex Drew."

Johnson made a note of the name.

"This is crap!" Humphries said. "John wouldn't just go missing."

"What was he wearing?" Johnson said.

"He was wearing a grey two-piece pinstripe suit when he got on the boat, but he took off his jacket, tie, shoes and socks on the way out. They're still on the boat, if you'd care to take a look."

"We'll certainly be doing that," Johnson said.

Humphries glanced up at the window. Water was running down the window in a continuous stream. "It would be suicidal to ask people to go out in this weather. Give me the coordinates and we'll start a search when the weather eases."

"I don't have the coordinates."

"Why don't you have them? The boat has sat nav."

"It isn't working."

Humphries was struggling to maintain his composure. "First you tell us the radio isn't working, and now you tell us the sat nav isn't working. Sat navs don't just not work, especially new ones. Lives depend on them. Why isn't it working?"

"How would I know? I'm not an engineer."

Johnson had a sudden thought. "Does Mrs McLaren know?"

"I haven't told her," Sybille said.

"This just gets worse," Humphries muttered.

"Why didn't you call her from your apartment?" Johnson said.

"I haven't been to my apartment," Sybille said. "I came straight ..."

"Are you sure about that?"

Sybille realised she had walked into a trap; the police must have been staking out the property. She tried to brazen it out. "Of course I'm sure," she said crossly. "I would know if I had been to my apartment, wouldn't I?"

"You would certainly know if you'd been telling us the truth," Johnson said. "But you're not telling the truth, Ms Johanssen, are you? You're lying to us. According to a report I received no more than forty-five minutes ago, you entered your apartment at 6:02 this evening, and you left again, to come here, at 7:38 p.m."

There was a loud fizzing sound followed immediately by an ear-splitting crack, followed by a flash of bright white light, followed by a clap of thunder that shook the building.

"Storm's right on top of us," Johnson said.

Sybille started to shake violently.

"You can stop the play-acting," Humphries said. "You're not fooling anyone."

"I'm not play-acting. I was struck by lightning as a child."

"Yeah, sure you were."

"All right, then. If you must know, I went to my apartment because I had a blinding headache and I needed a painkiller. And you lot would have a blinding headache if you'd had the day I've had. And I lay down to take a nap, and I overslept. I'm sorry. Okay?"

"When was John due to fly back to Florida?" Humphries asked.

"He was booked on an eight o'clock flight tonight. He was over just for the day."

Humphries checked his watch. "Well, that's something; Liz won't have started worrying yet." He took a notebook and pencil from his pocket. "Tell me the direction you were heading in, the speed you were travelling at, and how long it took you to get there."

"And give me the keys to your boat," Johnson said. "You can be our guest while we check it out."

Chapter 33

DCI Johnson suspected that Sybille's story was a complete fabrication.

Why, for example, would John McLaren fly over for a day of business talks, in a suit, and then suggest going out on the boat? And why would they have gone so far out? Surely, if he had wanted a trip on the boat, they would have taken a quick trip of, say twenty minutes to half an hour, and then gone to the property to talk. A boat trip of an hour and a half was hardly a trip; it was a fairly serious journey. And why would she choose to dive while he took a nap? And why for over an hour? How long does a nap last? And how do you find your way back when you're an hour and a half away, on water, without the assistance of satellite navigation? The answer: you don't.

Another reason he suspected her story was a fabrication was because of the way she told her story. Usually, when people are made to repeat their story a number of times, they tell it slightly differently each time they tell it. This is because each time they tell it they remember something they had not remembered before. He had made Sybille repeat her story four times, and, each time, she had told it in exactly the same way, using the same words, giving him the impression she had memorised, and rehearsed it. And the more she told it, the more her lack of passion, emotion and conviction came through. Later on in the proceedings, when she was telling it, she actually sounded bored. Most innocent folk go to considerable lengths to plead their innocence. Sybille had sounded as if it was just all too much trouble.

But, with no evidence of foul play, there was nothing Johnson could charge her with. As she had reminded him on three separate occasions during her four-hour interview, it was not a crime to report an accident.

While Sybille languished in a holding cell at the police station, two police vehicles converged on the marina. In one vehicle, a marked police car, were two uniformed officers and two detectives. In the other vehicle, an unmarked 4x4, were a police engineer, who was driving, and George Humphries.

Because the storm had coincided with a neap tide, the water in the marina was running several feet higher than usual, and several boats had found their way on to the car park.

John's boat was still on the water. It was pitching and tossing like something demented, but the lines were holding.

The drivers parked their vehicles in the lee of a cabin cruiser that was now occupying three parking spaces in the car park. They had brought arc lights and, after donning oilskin coats and hats, they set up the lights on a tripod by the boat.

When the lights were switched on, the water changed from an impenetrable black to translucent green. And Humphries spotted Sybille's name on the boat. He was incensed. John had told him about Sybille putting her name on the boat, but actually seeing it made Humphries' blood boil.

The arc lights swung to and fro in the wind and one of the uniformed officers elected to stay on the dock and hold the tripod steady.

The boat, which was still riding high in the water, did not appear to have suffered any damage above and beyond the hole in the bow.

There were cracking sounds as boughs broke off trees, and dull thuds as these hit the ground, and boats were breaking away from moorings and smashing into other boats in a scene reminiscent of a disaster movie. There was a strong smell of diesel.

Getting on board the boat required extreme care and split-second timing. The first man to attempt it, a uniformed officer, crouched and awaited his opportunity. When it came, he leapt aboard. He held on to the boat's rail, and extended a hand to help the next man aboard.

When everyone was on board, the engineer made his way to the centre console with George Humphries while the other men busied themselves photographing John's effects and looking for forensic evidence, although they realised there was little chance of finding forensic evidence in a boat in which an inch of water was sloshing around.

The engineer put the key in the ignition and turned it a quarter turn to the right. With the exception of the satellite navigation device and the ship-to-shore radio, the gauges on the centre console lit up immediately. It took the engineer all of thirty seconds to discover why the satellite navigation device was not working, and another thirty seconds to get it working.

"What was it?" Humphries yelled, the wind catching in his throat.

"A cable had been unscrewed."

"Could it have worked itself loose?"

"Not a chance. They screw these things tight. I reckon she had loosened it to finger tight earlier, and then unscrewed it with her fingers when she wanted to disable it."

Humphries straightened himself up and held on to the tee-top support as the boat lurched. He was mystified. "She must have used it to get back here from wherever they went, which means she must have disabled it when she got back. But why would she do that?"

The engineer shook his head. "Beats me. But then I'm just a simple engineer. Understanding the mind of a woman was never my strong point."

As to the ship-to-shore radio, the engineer discovered that the device did, indeed, have a fault.

Back in Orlando, Liz was unconcerned about John not getting home. She had seen a report on the storm on the evening news on TV and she knew that all flights had been cancelled and that the phone lines were down. She went to bed happy in the knowledge that he had found himself a hotel room and would call her as soon as he could.

Chapter 34

Liz was switching off her bedside lamp at the same time Sybille was leaving the police station. She had been told not to leave the island. This was ironic in the sense that the police had the keys to her boat and all flights to and from the island had been cancelled, and amusing in the respect that she had any number of contacts she could call on to get her off the island, regardless of the weather.

She was desperately tired and there was a nagging pain behind her eyes. She ran to her vehicle, getting soaked. She drove to the property and made a dash for her apartment. She stripped off her wet things and left them in a heap on her living room floor. She walked naked into her bedroom and put on her dressing gown.

She had had nothing to eat since breakfast, but she didn't feel particularly hungry so she dropped a couple of pieces of bread in her toaster and made herself coffee while she waited for the bread to toast.

Her breakfast dishes were still on the dining room table and she pushed them aside to make some room. She dunked her toast in her coffee. These days, if she ate anything other than soft food, her gums would bleed.

The pain behind her eyes was getting worse. She put her toast down and went into the bathroom and grabbed a handful of pills. She stuffed them in her mouth and cupped her hand under the cold water tap to wash them down. Eventually, the pain behind her eyes subsided. She climbed into bed a little after midnight, and lay awake almost until dawn.

When she finally dropped off to sleep, John's bloated body floated to the surface and leered at her. She woke with a start, bathed in sweat. Was there a message in the fact that this was the second time she had dreamt this? She switched on her bedside lamp and, comforted by the light, eventually drifted off to sleep again.

Chapter 35

'*And there's no news yet of the Englishman missing following a boating accident off Grand Bahama.*'

It was morning and Liz was watching the news on breakfast TV. She stared at the screen. She felt detached, as if this were happening not to her, but to someone else. Who else could it be, but John? And, if it were John, what was he doing on a boat? She realised she was missing what the newsreader was saying and dragged her eyes back to the screen. '*Because of high seas and storm force winds, all attempts to mount a search for him were postponed until six o'clock this morning. Bahamas Air and Sea Rescue are out looking for him as we speak.*'

She needed answers, and she needed them fast. She needed to call someone; someone close to where it happened, someone on the island. Her first thought was to call Jill, but then she realised that if it were John the newsreader was talking about, it was Sybille she needed to talk to because she was convinced that if anyone knew what had happened, it would be her.

She dialled the number of the property but got nothing but the dial tone. The lines must still be down. She left it for fifteen minutes, and then dialled again. She left it another fifteen minutes and dialled again, and then again. She was frustrated and needed air, so she went for a long walk.

When she got back, a cruiser in the livery of the Orlando Police Department was parked in the space allocated to the apartment. At the top of the steps leading to the apartment were two burly uniformed officers. One of them was pressing the doorbell; he had the chevrons of a sergeant on his sleeve.

Liz could hear the chimes from where she stood. Her heart sank. This had to be the worst kind of news. Hardly daring to breathe, she said, "Are you looking for me?" She was aware of a tremor in her voice.

"Are you Mrs John McLaren?" the sergeant asked.

"Yes, I am."

"Then could we have a word?"

Liz went weak at the knees and would have fallen if she had not grabbed the handrail for support.

The other officer stepped quickly towards the stairs. "Help you, ma'am?"

Liz lifted her hand to indicate she was all right. "It's my husband, isn't it?" Her voice was little more than a whisper.

"It might be better if we talked inside?" the sergeant said.

The kindness in his voice made Liz want to cry, and that was the last thing she wanted. She had to hold it all together. With an ever-increasing sense of dread, she mounted the stairs and began to climb. She got to the top of the stairs and let the two policemen into the apartment. She led the way into the living room. She desperately needed to know, but she was afraid to ask. Finally she blurted it out. "Have you come to tell me they've found his body?"

"No, ma'am," the sergeant said. "We probably don't know any more than you do."

Liz was confused. "Then why are you here?"

"Because the Freeport police have been trying to contact you. When they couldn't get a reply they asked us to come over and see if you were all right."

Liz felt an almost euphoric sense of relief. If they hadn't found his body, there was a chance he was still alive. She sighed, and then said, "Knowing her, I knew something like this would happen one day."

Sybille awoke to a loud rapping at the door to her apartment. Thinking it was a member of staff, she yelled, "Go away." She had a pounding headache.

The rapping began again.

"What is it?" she yelled.

"Police! Open the door."

"Of shit!" Sybille muttered. "I'm in bed," she yelled. "Can you come back later?"

The rapping began again.

"Okay, okay, keep your hair on," she muttered. "Give me a minute," she yelled. She climbed out of bed and groaned as she recognised the symptoms of a major hangover.

She slipped on her dressing gown and padded into the bathroom. She blanched when she saw herself in the mirror and pinched her cheeks to try and get some colour into them. She ran her fingers through her hair, tightened her dressing gown around herself, and headed for the door.

"Come on," DCI Johnson shouted. "We haven't got all day."

The damp clothes Sybille had taken off when she got back from the police station the previous evening were still in an untidy pile on the floor. She kicked them into a corner. Sunlight streamed in, momentarily blinding her, when she opened the door.

DCI Johnson was standing there with another man in a suit.

Sybille shielded her eyes from the sun. "Did you have to wake me so early?"

"I'd hardly call ten-thirty early," Johnson said. He introduced Sybille to his colleague.

"Good morning," DS Brewster said.

"What do you want?"

"We need to ask you some questions," Johnson said.

"For Christ's sake! You were asking me questions until midnight last night. What the hell else do you need to know?"

"We're going to keep asking you questions until we get at the truth. Now, are you going to let us in, or would you prefer to talk in front of your guests?"

It was checkout day and people were milling around.

"Wait there," Sybille said. "I'll get dressed."

"You'll do as you are," Johnson said. He pushed his way into the apartment.

Sybille let them in and then stepped out of the apartment to check what damage the storm had done. The buildings appeared to have survived without structural damage, which she was relieved about. Most of the damage seemed to be to the trees, and a quantity of sand had blow in from the beach. The gardener was using a long-handled net to drag the plastic garden furniture to the side of the pool from where he could lift it out of the water. She stepped back into the apartment and closed the door.

Johnson was standing in the living room wrinkling his nose. "This place smells like a Chinese laundry. Can we get some air in here?"

The air-conditioning was switched off and the room was stifling. Sybille marched across the room and flung open a window. A cooling breeze blew in. "That better?" she said, glaring at him. She gathered up the clothes she had kicked into the corner and tossed them into her bedroom. She closed the door, none too quietly, and threw herself into a chair. She did not invite them to sit.

They sat anyway.

"This is beginning to feel like police harassment," she said. "I told you everything I knew last night."

"In case you were wondering about the health and well-being of your business partner," Johnson said, his words dripping with sarcasm, "Bahamas Air and Sea Rescue are out there looking for him as we speak."

Sybille yawned, showing her contempt for her visitors by not bothering to cover her mouth. "Are the phone lines up again?"

Johnson glanced at his colleague in a can-you-believe-this? gesture. "How long did you say your sat nav had been out of action?"

"I didn't say. I don't know why you keep asking me that; I told you that at least three times last night."

"When did you last use your sat nav?" Brewster said.

"I don't remember. I told you that last night, too."

"What did you hope to gain by disabling it?" Johnson asked.

"Here we go again." Sybille was getting bored.

"Couldn't you have come up with something a bit more original than deliberately disabling the sat nav?" Johnson said. "Did you think we wouldn't find out? Do you think the police are stupid?"

Brewster didn't give Sybille time to comment. "Where were you on the night of June tenth, between midnight and two in the morning?"

Sybille looked at him pityingly. "Are you kidding? I can't even remember what I had for breakfast yesterday."

"The night of June tenth is rather more important than what you had for breakfast yesterday," Johnson said.

"I have no idea what I was doing that night." Sybille knew *exactly* what she had been doing that night.

"Why did you feel the need to install radar on the boat?" Brewster asked. They had deliberately not asked this question before.

"I didn't install radar. It was already ..." Sybille realised her mistake.

The detectives exchanged triumphant grins.

"It's the little things that catch people out," Johnson said. "We have the original bill of sale, and your partner did not pay for radar. So, let me ask you the question again; why did you feel the need to install radar?"

Sybille desperately needed a fix.

"And the fish boxes," Brewster said. "The boat looks as if it hasn't been cleaned since the day it left the factory, but the fish boxes have been cleaned, thoroughly, and within the last day or two. Now why would that be?"

"What are you suggesting?"

"We're not suggesting anything," Johnson said. "We're just trying to get at the truth."

Sybille got to her feet. "Listen, either charge me with something, or get the hell out of my apartment."

"All right, Sybille," Johnson said, taking his time to get to his feet. "We'll leave it there, for the moment. But you know the drill."

"I know, I know, don't leave the island." Sybille saw them to the door. "When do I get my boat back?"

"When I say you do," Johnson said.

Chapter 36

Liz booked herself on the next available flight to Freeport – the 4:00 p.m. departure from Orlando that day. Not knowing when she would be coming back, she left the return portion of her ticket open. She asked the airline to book her a room at one of their associate hotels and they phoned back to say they had booked her into the Princess Towers Hotel, which, paradoxically, was the hotel to which Sybille had invited her for coffee on the fateful day John had seen the property and thought it was exactly what he had been looking for. And now he was missing at sea.

Not knowing how long she was going to be away, Liz had no idea what to pack, but she steadfastly refused to believe that John was dead until such time as there was incontrovertible evidence to prove otherwise. She fervently believed he would turn up alive and well sometime, somewhere and, when he did, she wanted to look her best for him, so she packed the red dress he had bought her for her fiftieth birthday. She was zipping up her suitcase when the phone rang.

It was DCI Johnson. "How are you holding up?" he said.

"I'm fine," Liz said. She wasn't fine. How could she be fine? But she wasn't one to wear her problems on her sleeve. "Is there any news, Chief Inspector?"

"I'm afraid not. But I'm sure you'll be pleased to hear that George Humphries is overseeing the rescue operation personally."

"I am pleased. Bless him. By the way, Chief Inspector, thank you for having the Orlando police come to see me. It gave me comfort when I most needed it."

"You're welcome. We were frustrated that we couldn't get a message to you yesterday."

"I'm sure you were."

"As it happens, the Orlando police visiting you killed two birds with one stone, because they passed on everything you told them about your problems with Sybille Johanssen, some of which I was not previously aware of."

"I could fill a book on her."

"I'm sure you could. Are you planning to come to Freeport?"

"Yes, I am. I'm booked on a flight leaving Orlando at four o'clock this afternoon."

"Would you like me to send a car to the airport for you?"

"That won't be necessary, Chief Inspector, but thank you for the offer. I can take a taxi."

"Where will you be staying?"

"The airline has booked me a room at the Princess Towers Hotel. I should be comfortable there."

"Perhaps you'd call me when you get to the hotel, then I'll know you've arrived safely. Let me give you my direct phone number."

When her flight landed in Freeport, Liz took a taxi to the hotel. The female receptionist who checked her in could not have been more helpful, but as Liz walked to the lifts she picked up the phone.

Liz went to her room, unpacked her suitcase and hung her things. Then she phoned DCI Johnson. "I'm at the hotel," she said.

There was a click on the line. Liz thought the engineers were probably still working on the lines.

"How was your flight?"

"Very bumpy. They said it was clear air turbulence caused by the storm."

"It's because of turbulence that I dislike flying, although I do have to fly occasionally. It comes with the job."

"Is there any news, Chief Inspector?"

"Not yet, I'm afraid. I'll contact you as soon as I know something. If you're not in your room I'll leave a message with reception. Will nine in the morning be convenient? I'll send a car."

"Nine will be fine."

"It will be a marked police car and the driver will be in uniform. He'll ask for you by name at reception. Please don't get into any other car."

"It all sounds a bit cloak and dagger, Chief Inspector."

"Yes, I can see how it might, but all things considered, I don't think we can be too careful."

Liz spent the rest of the evening in her room. She kept the TV tuned to a 24-hour news channel and had her meal delivered by room service. She took a sleeping pill around ten p.m. and was asleep within minutes.

She slept through the sound of the key card sliding into the lock of her door in the early hours, and Sybille's muttered curse as the security chain tightened, and held.

Chapter 37

Liz woke up the next morning feeling lost and alone. She felt the need to have people around her, normal people, doing normal things, so she had breakfast in the hotel's busy restaurant.

There were four American men on the next table. They were dressed for golf and they were talking loudly about the courses they were going to play while they were on the island. One of them kept looking at her. She took it for a while and then felt like screaming: *You stupid man, I'm spoken for.* Despite being only half way through her scrambled eggs, she called for her bill and went back to her room.

She had left the TV on. It was set to the news channel she had been watching earlier. The news was repeated every few minutes. She sat and watched for a while, but there was no mention of John.

Ten minutes before the car was due, she ran a comb through her hair, touched up her lipstick and then took the lift down to the lobby.

A tall slim black man in the red and black uniform of the Bahamas Police Force stood in the middle of the lobby.

"Good morning, Mrs McLaren," the receptionist said. "Your driver's here." She waited until they had walked out of the building, and then picked up the phone.

At the police station, DCI Johnson rose from his desk. "Did you manage to get some sleep last night?"

"I slept very well as it happens. I took a sleeping pill. Is there any news, Chief Inspector? I've been watching the news on TV, but they seem to have dropped the story."

Johnson pointed to a chair and sat down at his desk. "They've had to call off the search."

Liz's eyes widened. "But why?"

"Because we don't know where to look. All we have is a general indication of where it happened. Air and Sea Rescue have searched the entire area, but he could be anywhere."

"But there was sat nav on the boat. Sybille must have known where it happened."

"She claims she didn't. And as to the sat nav, she had disabled it."

"Why would she do that?"

"We don't know. But the fact of the matter is, that without the coordinates, they don't know where to look. We've done everything but use thumb-screws on her, and we couldn't get her to tell."

"If I got her to give me the coordinates, would Air and Sea Rescue start the search again?"

"Without a doubt, but how would you propose to do that?"

"I have something she wants."

"But if she did give you the coordinates, how could you be sure she was giving you the right ones? We could be sending Air and Sea Rescue off on a wild goose chase again."

"Because I know this woman, Chief Inspector," Liz said, leaning forward in her chair and speaking earnestly. "I'll know if she's lying to me. Trust me on this."

"All right. How do you want to play it?"

"I'll call her and set up a meeting with her; just the two of us."

Johnson nodded. "All right. Use the phone in the interview room. I need to keep this phone free for incoming calls." He walked Liz to the interview room. "Dial nine to get an outside line. Come back to my office when you've finished."

Liz dialled the number of the property.

"Atlantic Beach Apartments. Gladys speaking. How may I help you?"

"Gladys, it's Mrs McLaren; John's wife. Is Sybille there?"

"Oh, Mrs McLaren. I'm glad you called. I'm so very sorry about John."

"Thank you. Is she there?"

"I'm afraid not. If you tell me where you are, I'll ask her to call you when she gets back."

"I'm staying at the Princess Towers hotel. Ask her to call me the moment she gets back, Gladys. I'll be in my room. Room 218. Please, it's most important."

Liz ended the call and walked back to Johnson's office.

Johnson was standing at his window looking at John's boat, which he had had taken off the water and brought here because, even though Sybille had given him the key and he had warned her not to leave the island, he didn't trust her not to have another key and take off to God knows where. When Liz walked in, he raised an eyebrow expectantly.

Liz remained on her feet. "She's not on the property. I've told the receptionist there to have her call me in my room the moment she gets back. So I'd better get back there."

Johnson picked up the phone. "I need a car. Now!"

Liz had been in her room no more than five minutes when there was a knock on the door. The bed had not yet been made and she thought it was probably the chambermaid. She opened the door.

"Surprise, surprise." Sybille was grinning like the proverbial Cheshire cat. She pushed past Liz and marched across the room and plonked herself on a chair.

Liz closed the door and sat on the edge of the bed, facing her.

"I see they haven't found him yet," Sybille said.

"When they don't know where to look, how can they find him?"

"Yes, that must be really irritating."

Sybille was smoking a cigarette. It was hand-rolled and, judging by the pungent aroma it was giving off, it was a spliff. Sybille blew a perfectly formed smoke ring.

A casual observer could have been forgiven for thinking that this was a meeting of old friends, since there was nothing in the body language of either woman to suggest otherwise. In point of fact, this was a one-on-one between two old adversaries and they were both motivated and on their mettle. Each had something the other wanted.

"It wasn't an accident was it, Sybille?"

"You tell me." Sybille blew another smoke ring.

"Is he dead, Sybille? Or have you got him squirreled away somewhere?"

"I certainly haven't got him squirreled away somewhere, as you put it. As to whether he's dead, I really couldn't say. Sorry."

"But you do know where it happened, don't you?"

"Do I?"

Liz resisted the urge to reach over and slap her, hard. "What would it take to get you to tell me where it happened?"

Sybille shrugged. "That would depend on what was in it for me."

"So you *do* know where it happened."

"At this stage, I'm not admitting anything."

"If I did make you an offer, how could I be certain you were giving me the correct coordinates?"

"You would just have to trust me, wouldn't you?" Sybille blew another smoke ring.

"Yes, but you're forgetting how well I know you."

"Then we seem to have reached a stalemate," Sybille said.

"What is it you want, Sybille?"

"What I've always wanted."

"Which is?"

"The property."

"And if I agree to give it to you?"

"But you wouldn't, would you? Not after all the money you and John have put into it."

"Don't judge everybody by your own standards, Sybille. Some things are more important than money. To some of us," she added pointedly.

Sybille thought for a moment, and then she said, "Lift up your top."

"Why should I do that?"

"Because I want to see if you're wearing a wire."

Liz lifted up her top. "Happy now?"

Sybille nodded. "Okay, if you agree to give me the property, I'll give you the coordinates."

"So you had them all the time."

"I wouldn't have been able to get there and back without them."

"But if we do a deal, how would you explain your suddenly remembering the coordinates to the police?"

"I'd probably say something along the lines that my memory plays tricks on me because of the drugs I take."

"And how would I know you were giving me the right coordinates?"

"Good question," Sybille said. "I can't tell you where John is, because I genuinely don't know where he is, but I can give you the coordinates for where I buried his effigy, and instructions on where to find it when you get there. I buried it where the boat was anchored when he went ... missing."

"What have you done with him, Sybille?"

"I've told you as much as I'm prepared to tell you."

"Just tell me one more thing: when you buried his effigy, how many pins were in it?"

"Five."

"Which is your limit, isn't it? When someone gets five pins in their effigy, something happens to them, doesn't it?"

"Does it?"

Liz sighed. "All right, Sybille, you win. The property's yours."

"I'll need a written agreement."

"Fine, have one drawn up. But I want the coordinates now; I mean immediately, otherwise the deal is off. "

"Do I have your word you'll sign it?"

Liz looked her in the eye. "Have you ever known me lie to you?"

"No, I don't believe I have."

"Well, then."

"I still need your word."

"Oh, for heaven's sake," Liz said impatiently. "I give you my word. There, now you have it. Now give me the coordinates, before I change my mind."

The phone on DCI Johnson's desk rang.

"I have the coordinates."

"I hope you didn't have to give away the shop, metaphorically speaking."

"She thinks I did. That's all that matters."

"I won't ask."

"No, best you don't know."

"George Humphries knows what's going on, and he's waiting for my call. I assume you'll want to go with them."

"You just try and stop me."

"Where are you now?"

"At the hotel."

"I'll send a car."

Chapter 38

George Humphries stood on the BASRA boat with two other men. The big diesel engine was clattering noisily.

The police car screeched to a halt and Liz leapt out.

Humphries helped her aboard and gave her a hug. He stepped back and looked into her eyes. "You okay?"

"I'm fine," Liz said. "Don't be nice to me, George, you'll make me cry."

"Did you bring the coordinates?"

Liz handed him a slip of paper. The coordinates were written in Sybille's childish scrawl.

"You're sure these are the right coordinates?"

"I'd stake my life on it."

Humphries handed the slip of paper to the man at the wheel, Jim Clancy, a broad-shouldered Bahamian in jeans and a T-shirt. "Let's go, Jim."

Clancy entered the coordinates into the boat's sat nav.

The engine throbbed as the boat pulled away from the dock.

The other man on the boat was DCI Johnson's colleague, DS Brewster.

Liz sat alone in the bow for the first part of the journey, partly because it was the quietest place on the boat and partly because she wanted to be alone with her thoughts, but then she made her way to the stern and sat with George Humphries, explaining to him about John's effigy, and Sybille's saplings.

"How did you get the coordinates out of her?"

"I had something she wanted," Liz said, not feeling the need to explain further.

When Clancy pointed to a line of trees seemingly sprouting from the ocean, Liz went and stood in the bow. Humphries went with her.

When they got close enough to make out the beach, and Clancy started to slow the boat down, Liz had to tell herself not to be silly when she felt an acute sense of disappointment that John was not standing on the beach, waiting to be rescued.

The storm had uprooted some trees, but Sybille's saplings were still standing. Liz pointed them out to Humphries, who, keeping one eye on the depth gauge and one eye on the saplings, guided Clancy in. When the depth gauge registered fifteen feet, he instructed Clancy to kill the engine. The anchor was tossed out.

If anyone had thought they might find something of interest in the water they were to be disappointed, because the water was about as murky as pea soup.

"This always happens after a storm," Humphries said. "The wind makes waves and the waves disturb the sand. It takes a few days for it to settle down again."

"I hope it doesn't mean we won't be able to find the effigy," Liz said anxiously.

"We *have* to find it," Brewster said. "Depending on what we find out here, this could be a crime scene. In which case we would need the effigy as evidence."

Clancy went below. He came up again wearing a swimming costume and carrying fins and a facemask. Humphries helped him strap on an air tank.

They followed Clancy's progress by watching the bubbles. He seemed to be working an area about fifteen feet square. He worked this area for ten to fifteen minutes, and then surfaced. He took another look at the saplings and then went down again and began to work an area closer to the beach.

Forty-five minutes after he had first entered the water, Clancy surfaced with the effigy in his hand.

"Good man!" Humphries called.

Clancy swam to the boat and handed the effigy to DS Brewster, who asked Liz as to the reason for the five pins.

"One for each time my husband did something Sybille hadn't want him to do," Liz said.

"I have to say that's a very well made effigy," Humphries said. "It actually looks like John. Now let's get on the island and see what else we can find."

They waited until Clancy had changed back into his jeans and T-shirt and then climbed into the inflatable dinghy they had been towing behind them. It had a small outboard motor and Humphries yanked the cord to start it.

They saw the footprints when they stepped out of the dinghy. There were three sets of them; all made by bare feet. One set had been made by someone they speculated as taking at least a size fourteen shoe.

"What size shoe does your husband take, Mrs McLaren?" DS Brewster asked.

"He takes an eleven," Liz said.

"I take an eleven," Humphries said. He was barefooted, like the rest of them, and standing close enough so as to make a comparison, yet far enough away so as not to disturb the other prints, he stood on one foot and allowed his weight to make an impression in the damp sand. He stepped away. His footprint was about the same length as the print he was comparing it with. "So that one looks like eleven. What do you think, Liz? Could John have made that set?"

Liz was frustrated. She wanted them to be John's, but she couldn't be sure. "They could be his, I suppose. But I've never had a reason to actually study his footprints."

"Is there anything unusual about your husband's feet, Mrs McLaren?" DS Brewster asked. "Does he have a particularly high instep, for example?"

"Well, now you mention it," Liz said, perking up, "there is something unusual about his feet. He's flat footed. So much so that the army turned him down. And there's another thing: his little toes curl under. He could never cut the nails on his little toes, because he couldn't get at them. I always cut them for him."

Brewster bent down low and studied one of the prints. "The little toe curls under on this one," he said. He looked at the print of the matching foot. "And so does this one." He straightened up again. "Well," he said, rubbing his hands together to get rid of the sand. "I think this is very encouraging."

The third set of prints was smaller and lighter, leading to speculation that they had probably been made by a woman.

Clancy put into words what the others were thinking. "I would say a boat with a woman and a big man on board put in to shelter from the storm and they found him and took him off with them when they left."

"Let's take a walk round the island and see if something else comes up," Humphries said.

They walked the length and breadth of the island, but found nothing else of interest. Humphries suggested they go back to the boat and cruise around for a while. "We won't find anything if we don't look," he said.

Back on the boat, Clancy turned on the engine, put the boat in gear and let it run on idle, which had the effect of moving them forward at the pace of a slow walk. They circled the island, and then circled it again, this time closer to the shore.

On their third pass the engine note suddenly changed and the boat lurched.

Humphries looked anxiously at Clancy. "Have we run aground, Jim?"

Clancy checked the depth gauge. "Don't think so. According to the depth gauge there's ten feet of water below us. Something must have fouled the propeller." He knocked the boat out of gear and turned off the engine. "I'd better take a look."

Shortly after Clancy had entered the water, the boat rocked. It rocked again, and then again. Clancy surfaced holding a pair of men's trousers. He swam to the boat and handed them to DS Brewster.

Liz recognised them immediately.

And did Brewster. "They're your husband's aren't they?"

"Yes, they are." Liz's voice was little more than a whisper.

"They're from the suit he was wearing," Brewster said. "I recognise the pinstripe from his jacket back at the office."

The propeller had done some damage to the trousers, but it was still immediately obvious that the belt and the button at the waistband had been undone, and the trousers unzipped.

"Well, one thing's for certain," Humphries observed dryly, "he was alive when he took his trousers off. Dead men don't undo their trousers."

Chapter 39

Sybille burst into Nicholas Truckle's office, unannounced and without knocking. She plonked herself down in a chair in front of his desk.

Truckle was working on an important document. He put his pen down and sat back in his chair and tried to conceal his annoyance at being interrupted.

"Guess what," she said gleefully. "I'm getting all Liz and John's shares in the property. I'll own it lock, stock and barrel."

The lawyer frowned. "You can't own it lock, stock and barrel? Enrico owns it."

Sybille clicked her tongue in annoyance. "Don't go getting all lawyerly on me. If I had their shares, and I paid him off, I would own it. Right?"

"Well, yes, I suppose you would. But …"

"Well then. I want you to draw up an agreement for me, and I want it yesterday."

The lawyer's patience was rapidly running out. "Sybille, you can't burst in here and expect me to drop everything, just because …"

"Oh, I think I can," Sybille said.

Something in Sybille's expression convinced the lawyer he should humour her until he knew more about what she had in mind. "It may seem like a stupid question, Sybille," he said, "but why would Liz hand over her and John's shares in the property when they've put all that money into it?"

"Because I had something she wanted."

"And may I make so bold as to ask what that was?"

Sybille hated it when the lawyer went pompous on her, but now was not the time to slap him down. She had a decision to make: should she tell him everything, or just enough to get him to draw up the agreement. She was itching to tell *someone*. She had heard of something called attorney-client privilege, which she believed to mean that whatever she told him could not be repeated. But before she said anything, she needed to be certain. "Whatever I tell you is covered by attorney-client privilege. Right?"

"Well, yes," the lawyer replied cautiously.

"Which means you can't pass on anything I tell you. Right?"

"Well, yes."

"What do you mean, *well yes*? Does it, or does it not?"

"All right, yes it does." The lawyer chose not to reveal that, should he suspect that something of a criminal nature had taken place, he was duty bound to inform the police.

Satisfied she was on safe ground, Sybille said, "Right, then I'll tell you. I gave Liz the coordinates in exchange for her and John's share of the property."

The lawyer could scarcely believe his ears. What Sybille was telling him was plumbing new depths, even for her. "You mean you knew all along where John went missing?"

"Of course I did. I was there, wasn't I?"

"You let Air and Sea Rescue go out not knowing where to look, in weather like *that*?"

"Oh, don't be so bloody melodramatic."

"Was it an accident, Sybille?"

Sybille did not respond. She realised she had said enough already.

The lawyer sat up straight in his chair. "Sybille, if I think something of a criminal nature has occurred, I am obliged to inform the police. Despite attorney-client privilege."

"But you wouldn't, would you?" A smile played on Sybille's lips.

The implied threat, together with Sybille's general demeanour, was making the lawyer nervous. He wanted to get this over with and get her out of his office. "What is it you want, Sybille?" he said.

Sybille had brought with her a sheet of scribbled notes. She handed it to him. "I want you to draw up an agreement based on this. Liz promised to sign it."

When the lawyer read the notes, he realised that Liz had set Sybille up. And, all things considered, he didn't blame her. He found himself between a rock and a hard place. He knew Sybille wouldn't leave until he agreed to draw up an agreement, and he also knew he was in possession of compulsive evidence as to Sybille's complicity in whatever had happened to John. "I need time to think about this, Sybille," he said.

Sybille played her trump card. "Would it help you think about it if I told you I know about the drugs deal you and Enrico did ten years ago? What was it you netted out of it? Three million dollars each? And how many policemen were killed? Three, wasn't it?"

The colour drained from the lawyer's face. "How long have you known?"

Sybille shrugged. "About three years, give or take. I got wind of it from one of the guys involved. All it took was a night in the sack to get the details out of him. You've been a very naughty boy, Nicholas."

The lawyer tried to brazen it out. "Knowing something, and proving it, can be two very different things, Sybille."

Sybille smiled. "Try me."

"It happened a long time ago."

"What difference does that make?"

The lawyer slowly shook his head. "You've been sitting on this all this time, haven't you? Biding your time."

"And it paid dividends, didn't it? So what's it to be, your career and your freedom, or my agreement?"

"All right, Sybille," Truckle said quietly. "You'll get your agreement. Stop by at nine in the morning. I'll have it ready for you."

Chapter 40

The BASRA boat got back to Freeport a little after 7:00 p.m.

When Clancy had shut down the engine, Liz gave him a peck on the cheek. "Thank you, Jim. Thank you for everything."

Clancy beamed. "My pleasure. I'm sure your husband will turn up soon."

Humphries helped her ashore and then checked his watch. "Jill told me to invite you for dinner tonight," he said, "but it's late and you have to go to the police station yet. Why don't we make it tomorrow night?"

"Tomorrow would be fine," Liz said. "I would be too tired tonight. It's been an exhausting day."

"Pier One okay?"

Liz smiled. "Pier One would be perfect."

"I'll book a table. We'll pick you up around seven."

In the police car on the way to the police station, Liz sat holding John's trousers. She was oblivious to how damp they were.

Brewster got a slap on the back from his boss when he escorted Liz into DCI Johnson's office. "Great result, Fred."

"Thanks," Brewster said, sheepishly trying to hide his pleasure at the accolade. "I'll get on with my report. I'm glad it worked out so well, Mrs McLaren."

"So am I, Fred. And thank you. I'm glad you came."

"It seems you were right when you said you could get her to give you the coordinates," Johnson said, indicating a chair.

Liz perched herself on the edge of the chair.

"Well," Johnson said, sitting down again at his desk, "it seems you were right again."

"I told you, Chief Inspector. I know this lady."

"So it would seem. It will be interesting to see how she explains suddenly remembering the coordinates."

Liz handed him the trousers.

The jacket to the suit was hanging over the back of a chair and Johnson held the trousers against it to compare them. "Not much doubt about that," he said. "We've got an all-points bulletin out, and I'm sure John will turn up soon."

"What are you going to do about *her*, Chief Inspector?" Liz couldn't bring herself to mention Sybille's name.

"Well, since there's no evidence of an actual crime, there's not much we can do. It might be a different story when John turns up and tells us what happened."

Liz yawned, covering her mouth with her hand.

"You look tired, Mrs McLaren. Why don't I have a car drive you to your hotel?"

"That would be nice, Chief Inspector. I *am* tired."

When Liz got to her room, the first thing she did was run herself a hot bath. She filled it to within a few inches of the brim and used two sachets of the hotel's bubble bath, feeling she had the right to spoil herself. She took off her clothes and draped them over a chair in the bedroom and then padded into the bathroom and climbed into the bath. As she luxuriated in the heat and the silky feel of the water, her eyelids began to droop and she fell asleep.

She awoke with a start when there was a bang that rattled the hinges on the door to her room.

"It's Sybille," a voice called loudly. "I want a word. Come on, I know you're in there."

There was another bang. "Come on, open the door."

Liz climbed out of the bath and wrapped herself in a bath towel. She stepped into the bedroom. "What is it, Sybille?" she called.

"I want to talk to you."

"Well, I don't want to talk to you. I've nothing to say to you."

There was another bang.

Liz had had enough. She marched across the room, picked up the phone and dialled zero to get the hotel operator. "There's someone trying to break into my room."

"Hang up, Mrs McLaren," the operator said. "But stay by the phone. I'll send a security guard."

Liz dried herself with the towel and then slipped into the fluffy cotton bathrobe the hotel provided.

There was another bang and then the sound of heavy footsteps running down the corridor. A man's deep voice boomed. "Yo, lady, quit kickin' that door!"

"I just want to talk to her."

"Well, I guess she don't want to talk to you."

There was another bang.

"That's it, lady. You're outta here."

"Get your hands off me, or I'll have the law on you."

"Around here, lady, I *am* the law."

There was a knock on the door. "This is security, ma'am. You okay?"

"I'm fine," Liz called.

Sybille's complaining voice tailed off as she was led away.

Liz had not eaten since breakfast and she was ravenous. She ran her eyes over the room service menu and ordered herself a turkey club sandwich and coffee with milk. Thinking her meal would take a half hour or so, she lay on the bed and closed her eyes. She dozed off.

She awoke to a loud rapping at the door. She sat bolt upright, her heart pounding.

A female voice called, "Room service."

It didn't sound like Sybille, but Liz was taking no chances. "Just a second," she called. She rolled off the bed and walked to the door. "What did I order?" she called.

"Ma'am?"

"What did I order for my meal?"

"A turkey club sandwich, and coffee with milk."

Liz opened the door, leaving the security chain in place.

A pair of black eyes stared back at her. Liz recognised the young woman as a waitress in the hotel's restaurant. She was holding a tray at shoulder level. Liz released the security chain and opened the door. "Sorry," she said. "I had someone try to break into my room earlier. I thought she might have come back again."

"No, ma'am, she's gone. The manager threw her out and told her that if she ever set foot in the hotel again he would call the police."

Chapter 41

When Liz woke up the next morning, she decided it would be prudent to stay within the confines of the hotel until John turned up. Sybille shouldn't be able to get at her there. And, rather than spending the day in her room, the pool area – which always seemed busy, seemed like a sensible option. Even if Sybille got past the security guards, she was unlikely to try anything with scores of people milling around.

She called DCI Johnson before going down to breakfast to let him know where he could find her if John turned up. While she was on the phone to him she told him about Sybille trying to break into her room.

"Thank you for letting me know," he said. "The situation would seem to be contained for the moment, but let me know if anything else happens."

"I will. If you hear from John, Chief Inspector…"

"You'll be the first to know."

Several coach loads of people had just arrived off a flight from Toronto and the lobby was heaving. Liz picked her way through a mess of people, luggage and golf bags and made her way to the restaurant.

She took her time over breakfast, chatting with an American couple who were having breakfast on the next table with their two young children. The children were giggling at Liz's English accent. She finished her breakfast, wished the young couple an enjoyable holiday, signed her bill and went back to her room.

She was flicking through a magazine when the phone rang. She let it ring, thinking it might be Sybille. And then, realising she was getting paranoid about Sybille, she picked up.

"Hi there," a cheerful voice said.

"Oh, it's you, Jill. Sorry for not picking up; I thought it might be Sybille."

"Not her again. What's she been up to now?"

There was a click on the line.

"She tried to break into my room last night."

"She *what*? The woman needs locking up. Liz, I realise you are probably expecting John to turn up at any time, but I didn't want you to have to spend the day on your own. I can be there in fifteen minutes. We can go somewhere nice. Do some shopping. Whatever."

"It's very sweet of you, Jill, but I thought I'd hang around the hotel. I've told the police where I am, in case John turns up, and Sybille can't get at me here."

"Understood. But listen, sweetie, call me if you need me, or if you get tired of your own company. Okay?"

"I will."

"Liz, I also called to tell you we've booked a table at Pier One for eight o'clock this evening. We'll pick you up at seven-thirty."

"Good, I'm looking forward to it. What are you planning to wear?"

Sybille waltzed into the reception area of Nicholas Truckle's law firm and, ignoring a very frosty look from the receptionist, headed for the double doors leading to the inner sanctum.

The receptionist, an English spinster and a stickler for protocol, got to her feet. "Excuse me," she said loudly. "You can't go in there."

Sybille broke stride and glared at the woman. "Who the hell do you think you're talking to?"

Clients sitting waiting to see their lawyers looked up and started to take an interest.

"I'm talking to *you*."

"Do you know who I am?"

"Yes, I know who you are."

Sybille told herself to stay calm. "Nicholas told me to drop in this morning," she said. "There should be an agreement waiting for me."

"And there is, but you're not to go in there." She stepped nimbly past Sybille and stood between her and the doors with her back to the doors.

Sybille blinked at the woman's effrontery. "Who says I'm not to go in there?"

"Mr Truckle has left instructions that you are to be handed the agreement, but that you are not to otherwise be allowed in."

Sybille and the receptionist were now centre stage. Whatever reason the clients had had for coming to see their lawyer was, for the moment, forgotten.

"I see," Sybille said. "Then perhaps would you get him on the phone for me, because I'd like a word with him."

"He doesn't want to speak to you on the phone, either."

"Where's my agreement?" Sybille said.

The receptionist took an A4-size manila envelope from a shelf under the semi-circular desk and handed it to her. It had Sybille's name on it and it was marked Private and Confidential.

"Thank you," Sybille said. "Will you give Nicky a message for me?"

"Of course."

"Will you ask him how the fuck he is going to enjoy spending the next twenty years of his life in jail?" Sybille turned on her heel and swept from the room.

A blush appeared at the base of the receptionist's neck and it spread rapidly to her throat and then to her cheeks. She smiled weakly at the onlookers and hurried through the double doors. When she walked into Nicholas Truckle's outer office, his secretary looked up in surprise.

"Good gracious, Angela," she said. "You're the colour of beetroot. Is something wrong?"

"That dreadful Johanssen woman just came in to pick up the agreement you left for her and, when I wouldn't let her in to see Nicholas, she asked me to give him a message."

"He's busy at the moment, Angela. If you give me the message, I'll make sure he gets it."

"Actually, Anne, I think I should give it to him myself."

The look on her colleague's face was enough to convince Anne this was not the time to argue. "Just a second, Angela. I'll see if he can see you." Anne got to her feet, knocked on Truckle's door and walked in.

The lawyer frowned. "I told you I didn't want to be disturbed, Anne."

"I'm sorry, Nicholas, but Sybille Johanssen has left a message with Angela for you."

"I see," the lawyer said slowly. "And the message?"

"Angela was too embarrassed to tell me. She said she thought she should tell you herself."

The lawyer took off his reading glasses and laid them carefully on his desk. "Very well. Ask her to come in."

Angela walked in, her face on fire.

"I understand you have a message for me, Angela."

"I'm sorry, Nicholas, but you're not going to like…"

"Just tell me what she said, Angela."

Angela swallowed. "She said to ask you how the … er …how the fuck you'll enjoy spending the next twenty years in jail."

The lawyer nodded. "I see. Thank you, Angela. Please close the door on your way out." For the next few minutes Truckle paced his office, deep in thought. He had a very important decision to make; probably the most important decision of his entire life. Finally, he returned to his desk and sat down and picked up the phone. "Anne, get the police on the phone, please. There's something I need to talk to them about."

Chapter 42

A grossly overweight woman wearing garish Bermuda shorts was talking to Gladys when Sybille marched into the office.

"Beautiful day, Sybille," Gladys said.

Sybille scowled. "Fuck the weather!" She elbowed the overweight woman aside and headed for the phone on the desk. "What's Pier One's number?"

Gladys checked the number in her card index system and wrote it down on a Post-It note.

Sybille picked up the phone and dialled the number. "Uwe, it's Sybille." Her brow darkened. "What do you mean, Sybille who? Sybille Johanssen. What? Yes, I'm fine. Listen, I understand George Humphries has a table for three booked tonight. What? What does it matter how I know? I just do. Will you stop interrupting me? I want the table next to his." She listened to what the restaurant manager had to say, and then said, "Your balcony's always fully booked, but you gave George Humphries a table at short notice. As I see it, there's no reason why you can't give me one." She listened again. "No, a table inside the restaurant will not do. Jesus, why do you have to make it so difficult?" She listened again. "I don't give a flying fuck how busy you are, I want that table. Let me spell it out for you, Uwe, you either give me that table, or I'll burn the place down. That's better. Thank you. I'll have a dinner guest, and he's a VIP, so make sure you treat him like one."

That afternoon, DCI Johnson spent an enlightening few hours with Nicholas Truckle, following which he instructed the lawyer to surrender his passport.

And a warrant was issued for the arrest of Sybille Johanssen.

Chapter 43

When Sybille and her dinner guest got to Pier One they had, to Sybille's considerable annoyance, to stand in line on the staircase with everyone else. She was carrying an A4-size manila envelope.

Uwe was in his usual place: at his station at the top of the stairs. He was admitting people with reservations, and turning away those without. He greeted Sybille with a small bow and a polite, "Good evening, Sybille."

"Am I getting the table I asked for?" Sybille demanded.

"Of course," Uwe said smoothly.

Sybille's dinner guest had the air of a man used to getting his own way. He looked to be in his late fifties, early sixties. He was impeccably dressed. When Uwe greeted him and welcomed him to Pier One, he merely nodded.

Uwe picked up a couple of menus. "If you'd like to follow me."

Liz was sitting at a table by the balcony rail with George and Jill Humphries. She was laughing at something Humphries had said. Her smile froze when she saw Sybille.

Sybille stopped beside her and smirked. "Well, fancy meeting you here."

Liz clucked in annoyance and looked the other way.

Sybille laughed. "Have it your way, but we'll be talking later. You can bet on that." When she got to her table, her guest had already sat down. Sybille sat down and Uwe handed them menus and started to go into his spiel about the specials of the day.

Sybille let him finish, and then said, "We're in no hurry. We'll have a drink before we decide."

"I'll send the waiter over," Uwe said.

Humphries caught Uwe's sleeve as he walked past their table. "Uwe," he said quietly, "do you have another table? I'd rather we weren't sitting next to that woman."

"I'm sorry, Mr Humphries," Uwe said. "All my tables are taken."

"If it's me you're worried about, George," Liz said, "don't be. She can't get up to any mischief with you and all these other people around. It's all right, Uwe, we're fine where we are."

Uwe signalled a waiter and pointed to Sybille's table, and then went back to his station. He showed two more parties to their tables and came back to find a tall broad-shouldered man dressed in sailing gear, which seemed oddly too big for him, and a Boston Red Sox baseball cap pulled low over his eyes and dark sunglasses.

"Good evening, sir. Do you have a reservation?"

"I didn't come to eat," the man said. "I just came to see the show, if that's all right." His accent sounded English.

Uwe had the impression he had met him before, but he couldn't think where. "Of course, it is. Why don't you have a drink in the bar while you wait? I ring a ship's bell when the show's about to start. Our bartender does a wonderful Bahama Mama. "

"Thank you," the man said.

Liz was about to make a start on her lobster thermidor when Sybille tapped her on the shoulder. She turned irritably. "What is it, Sybille?"

Sybille thrust the manila envelope at her. "Read it and sign it."

Taken by surprise, Liz took the envelope. "What is it, for heaven's sake?" So much had happened in the last thirty-six hours that she had completely forgotten she had promised Sybille she would sign an agreement.

"Don't give me that crap," Sybille said. "You know perfectly well what it is. You promised to sign it, so sign it."

Now Liz remembered. "I'm not signing anything," she said. She tossed the agreement back. "Now leave me alone."

Sybille's dinner guest represented a Colombian drug baron who wanted to set up a distribution operation in the Bahamas. Sybille had persuaded him that the property would provide excellent cover. "The deal's off if she doesn't sign," he said.

"Trust me," Sybille said. "I've never known her not do something she promised to do. Did you bring the money?"

The Colombian nodded. "Seven hundred thousand dollars, in cash, as agreed."

Sybille frowned. "We agreed seven-fifty."

"There have been, shall we say, expenses."

Sybille knew she was being ripped off. She also knew there was nothing she could do about it. "What time's the boat picking me up?"

"0100 hours tomorrow. And they won't wait."

DCI Johnson wanted to pick Sybille up mob-handed, because he didn't want her slipping through his fingers, but there was a manpower shortage and he could only get the number of uniformed officers he wanted at nine p.m. He wasn't unduly concerned, because the unmarked Chevrolet was at the property.

Due to a foul-up in communication, however, the Chevrolet was not where it should have been when Sybille left the property with her escort at eight p.m.

Johnson arrived at the property with five uniformed officers in two marked police cars at 9:15 p.m. He ordered his men to their positions and went straight to Sybille's apartment. DS Brewster was with him.

Sybille had left a light burning in her living room. She did this out of habit. Burglaries were rife in the Bahamas and she believed someone intent on breaking in would be discouraged if they saw a light. Not that she had anything worth stealing.

Johnson saw the light and thought she was in. He hammered on the door. "Police! Open the door!" There was no reply. He hammered again. "Come on, Sybille. We know you're in there."

The overweight woman Sybille had elbowed out of the way earlier in the day heard the commotion and stepped out of the adjoining apartment. "Try Pier One," she said. "And do me a favour, when you catch the bitch throw away the key."

The lights were on in the main body of the restaurant and the citronella candles had been replaced on the tables on the balcony. It was a balmy evening with barely enough breeze to cause a flicker in the flame.

Uwe appeared with a box of frozen bait. He rested the box on the balcony rail and flicked the switch to turn on the underwater lights. A swathe of pale green light sprang to life under the water. He rang the ship's bell eight times: clang clang; clang clang; clang clang, clang clang.

The bell, which was no more than five feet from Liz's left ear, almost deafened her.

There was a mad scramble for the balcony as people rushed from the main body of the restaurant to watch the show.

Liz pushed her chair back and got to her feet. She had seen the show on a number of occasions, but it was always worth watching.

Sybille, who had been sitting with her back to Liz, heard Liz's chair move. She picked up the agreement, jumped to her feet and moved to the rail.

They stood side by side, their shoulders touching.

There was nothing Liz could do about it. There was such a crush of people there was barely enough room to breathe, let alone move.

Uwe grabbed a handful of bait and tossed it over the rail. He tossed over another handful, then another. Then he upended the box, sending the balance of the contents splattering into the water.

Shoals of little fish appeared, in waves like underwater smoke, and began attacking the bait.

The crowd parted to allow Uwe to get another box of bait. He came back and tipped it in the water. He went back for a third box.

The barracuda moved in, large and menacing. They lay by the perimeter of the light, watching their prey. Flashes from cameras on the balcony illuminated the darkness.

When they moved in for the kill, the barracuda moved in like arrows raining on a circle of covered wagons. The water boiled as the feeding frenzy upped its pace.

A dorsal fin appeared from out of the darkness.

Someone yelled, "There's one."

Someone else yelled, "And there's another one."

Soon a dozen or more sharks were circling.

Over the din came the sound of approaching sirens.

At first, the sharks circled unhurriedly, as if they were just there to watch. But suddenly they launched themselves into the melee. There were shrieks of delight from the balcony as their teeth ripped into their prey.

The sirens were getting louder.

Sybille thrust the agreement at Liz. "Here, sign it."

Liz grabbed the agreement and tossed it over the rail. "I'm not signing anything, you stupid woman! He's still alive!"

"Oh, shit!" Sybille leaned over the rail and tried to grab the agreement.

And a hand came from behind and pushed her ...

THE END